KU-865-010

STONE COLD RED HOT

Private eye Sal Kilkenny is asked to discover the whereabouts of Jennifer Pickering, disinherited by her family twenty years ago. However, it seems that Jennifer does not want to be found, although her brother Roger is determined to find his sister – their mother is dying and he craves an emotional reunion to bury their differences. As the events of the past unfold, single-mum Sal finds she is becoming engrossed in the mystery, even against her better judgement. There are dark secrets waiting to be uncovered, but can Sal break the conspiracy of silence that surrounds the case?

STONE COLD RED HOT

STONE COLD
RED HOT

by

Cath Staincliffe

Magna Large Print Books
Long Preston, North Yorkshire,
BD23 4ND, England.

British Library Cataloguing in Publication Data.

Staincliffe, Cath
    Stone cold red hot.

    A catalogue record of this book is
    available from the British Library

    ISBN   0-7505-1875-8

First published in Great Britain in 2001
by Allison & Busby Limited

Copyright © 2001 by Cath Staincliffe

Cover illustration © Anthony Monaghan

The right of Cath Staincliffe to be identified as the author of this work has been asserted by her in accordance with the Copyright, Designs and Patents Act, 1988

Published in Large Print 2002 by arrangement with
Allison & Busby Limited

All Rights reserved. No part of this publication may be reproduced, stored in a retrieval system, or transmitted in any form or by any means, electronic, mechanical, photocopying, recording or otherwise without the prior permission of the Copyright owner.

Magna Large Print is an imprint of Library Magna Books Ltd.

Printed and bound in Great Britain by
T.J. (International) Ltd., Cornwall, PL28 8RW

0466235

For Daniel, Ellie and Kit

Acknowledgements

Many thanks to Sean Duffy, Annie Manogue and Paul Morris who helped me with information on neighbour nuisance units, housing policy and Somali nomenclature. Any diversion from usual custom and practice is down to me. And as ever thanks to the novel writing group: Fay, Julia, Maggie and Natasha, for invaluable support and feedback.

Chapter One

My first impression of Roger Pickering was of nervous tension. He stood on the doorstep, hiding behind his fringe of light brown hair, eyes cast anywhere but at me.

'Sal Kilkenny?' He managed to get my name out.

'Yes, Mr Pickering. Please come in.'

I led him along the hall and downstairs to my office in the cellar. With the self-absorption of the painfully shy, he made no small talk, no comment on our location and politely refused coffee.

I had told him about the Missing Person's Helpline, when he had first rung me. He'd tried that, he said, a year ago when it became obvious his mother wouldn't get better. Nothing had come of it. No word. Just a resounding silence. Like the silence that had echoed through their home for the past twenty three years. Since the day his sister left.

'We never talk about it,' he said. 'Like it never happened.'

'Do you know whether she ever got in touch?'

He shook his head, shrugged. 'I don't think so but I've no idea really. Something happened but they'd never talk about it, wouldn't even mention her name.' His forehead creased as he fished for accurate recollections. 'I think at first they told me she'd gone to university but later they said she'd left her course. They said she wouldn't be coming back. She was a disgrace. I remember my mother using those words, a disgrace. But I never knew why.'

'How old were you?'

'Eight,' he blinked rapidly, 'my parents were always strict. They were getting on in years when they had Jennifer and when I arrived, ten years later, they were even older. They never...' he searched for the right words, '...they didn't talk about things. Everything was proper and if it wasn't then you certainly didn't dwell on it. And you didn't tell the children. Old fashioned really. Stiff upper lip and all that,' he smiled.

'Have you asked them? Recently?'

He perched on the edge of his seat as we talked, his face never still. He had a pleasant face, boyish, though he was in his early thirties by my reckoning, hazel eyes with dark lashes, pale skin which emphasised the red of his lips.

'Last year,' he glanced up at me from beneath his fringe, 'well – I tried. It was awful. It was my mother I asked. My father's dead now. She, she just acted like I hadn't spoken. Completely ignored me. And when I repeated myself, asked her to tell me why Jennifer had never been home then she got really angry. She lost her temper and started talking about how I'd promised never to mention that name in this house again and had I no respect for her feelings and then she started crying. She never cries,' his face told me how uncomfortable he'd been. 'I had to leave it alone.'

'So, what does she think of you hiring a private detective to find your sister?'

'She doesn't know.'

Heigh ho. 'She may have to.'

His eyes widened.

'It might be possible to trace your sister without talking to your mother. She's going to have a lot more information about where Jennifer may have gone, who her friends were, all that. Missing persons can be very hard to trace without good leads. Where would I start? Do you know what university

13

she went to?'

'No.'

'Can you remember who her friends were?'

'There was one I remember, Lisa, she lived at the old vicarage. The others ... there was a Carol, I think.'

'But your mother would know where she lived and what her surname was, wouldn't she?'

'I don't want you to talk to her,' assertive in spite of his nervousness.

'Sometimes people will open up more easily to a stranger, you know. They're not losing face in the same way, there's no shared history of how things have to be.'

'No, not yet. If it becomes impossible, like you say then maybe ... but can't you just try first? I'm sure there are some things I can find out – names of people you could talk to, that sort of thing.'

'OK. You see, I really do need an idea of whereabouts to look – I can try electoral rolls for example but do I start in Manchester or London or Edinburgh? Without an area to focus on it's a waste of time, to be honest.'

'But if I got you the names of her old friends, people who might know where she could have gone…'

'Yes, that would help. However from what you've said, it sounds as though your mother wouldn't want to see Jennifer even if we did trace her.'

'I know,' he stared at the floor, 'but it's not just that. It's true, I think Jennifer has a right to know that Mother's dying and she should be able to try and make contact if she wants, to write or call, before it's too late. But there's the house as well, you see. Jennifer will be entitled to half of it, and there's money left from Father's estate.'

'You want her to get her share of the inheritance?' Not all siblings were so generous.

'Yes. And I want to find her. Whatever went on, all those years ago, it had nothing to do with me. I was eight years old, I lost my sister. But I'm not a child anymore, I want to know where she is and how she's getting on. I can remember feeling scared. I thought that maybe I'd done something to make her leave. And then I was cross, for a long time: she didn't care about me, never even sent a note. After that I suppose I got used to the idea, forgot about it more or less. But this last couple of years I've been wondering about her, it's become important. Not just because of mother but for me.' His eyes flicked up at me and away. 'We don't need to carry on as we have been. She's all the family I have – once Mother's gone.' He reddened as he concluded. There was no self-pity in his tone; instead I could hear determination, bravery too.

'OK. I need as many facts and figures, names and addresses as you can dredge up. Neighbours, friends, teachers, relatives, boyfriends. Get a photo as well – that's very important. When I've got all that I'll start by talking to her old friends, try and establish which university it was, try doing a document search there. They may have a record of where she went once she left. Sometimes an ad in the local paper is all it needs.'

He grinned, delighted at the prospect of hope.

'But then after twenty-three years, she may well have moved around… If you come back in, what … two days time with those details? For now I need her full name.'

'Jennifer Lesley Pickering.'

'Date of Birth?'

'Same day as mine; 4th March 1958.'

'You had the same birthday?'

'Yes. And after she'd gone it felt so weird. I'd be opening my presents and it was so

16

obvious that she was missing but no-one referred to it.'

'She never sent a card?'

'No,' his shoulders slumped slightly.

That seemed cruel. Or had his parents intercepted mail?

'Had you been close?'

'Not really. It was such a big age gap. She played with me when I was little but then she was busy with school and friends and I suppose I had my own friends.'

'Tell me about her – what was she like?'

He sat back in the chair for the first time since he'd arrived. 'I can't remember a lot. She was lively, noisy I suppose. I can remember her arguing with my father at the tea table, getting sent to her room, going on about what a mess the world was in, teenage stuff like that. She was full of energy. That was why it felt so quiet when she'd gone. If she was in a good mood she'd let me sit in her room while she got ready to go out or if she was just messing about. She always had the radio on. Radio Caroline,' he smiled suddenly, 'she told me it was a pirate station and I'd this image of Captain Pugwash and Long John Silver playing music. I couldn't figure it out. She had friends round some-times but she went out more, I think their places were probably more easygoing.'

'Friends from school?'

'Yes. Oh, and there was a big place, I can't remember the name, I'll check it for you, it was a banqueting place, they did conferences and dinner dances and weddings. Jennifer used to waitress, there was a whole crowd of them did it at the weekends.'

'What was she studying at university?'

'English, I think.'

That hardly narrowed it down.

'And she left home in the autumn?'

'This time of year,' he agreed. 'For the new term, I suppose. I don't know if it was September or October. I was back at school. I wanted to go see her off on the train but one day I got in from school and my mother said she'd left for university. I felt so disappointed. Mainly about the train,' he said ruefully.

'And it was sometime after that they told you she'd left the university?'

'Yes, I think I must have kept asking about her and that's when they told me that and said she was a disgrace.'

'What do you think happened?'

He took a breath. Looked across at the large, blue abstract painting on my wall. 'I think she got pregnant. I can't think of anything else that would have made them cut her off like that.'

Oh, I don't know – coming out as a lesbian maybe or moving in with a boyfriend might have had a similar effect on the narrow minded – we were talking nearly a quarter of a century ago. Pregnancy seemed a pretty good bet though, good as any at this stage.

He carried on. 'My mother still has a bee in her bonnet about marriage. I've friends at work who aren't married and have children and she thinks it's appalling.'

'Is she very religious?'

'Yes. She doesn't get to church anymore but she keeps in touch. Her father was a lay-preacher. Very puritanical. Their church was connected to the Methodists but they were much stricter. All about rules and the proper conduct of a respectable life. "The right and proper way",' he quoted. 'They had a hill-farm up in the Yorkshire Dales, I think most of the surrounding farms joined the church. Like a separate community in a way.'

'And your father?'

'That's how they met. He'd been to university and studied accountancy. Then the war broke out and he joined up. He was an officer. He returned to one of the army camps up in Yorkshire and got involved with the church, met my mother there. After he left the army he set up as an accountant in Manchester and they got married. They established a congregation here, he became the leader. He was very conservative. He thought we should still have National Service, wanted to bring back hanging and preserve the Empire.' He laughed nervously. Speaking ill of the dead? 'It wasn't all stern lectures though. He loved to garden. We'd help him. It was the one time we all seemed to be happy together.'

My heart softened pathetically. I was a fellow gardener. I resisted the temptation to start blethering on about planting schemes and pests and diseases and carried on making notes.

'So he had his own business?'

'A firm, yes. They did very well. He prided himself on their reputation.'

'And your mother looked after the house and the two of you?'

'Oh, yes. A woman's place was definitely in the home.'

'Did they encourage Jennifer to go to university?'

'Yes, I think so. That would have been something to be proud of, a good education, qualifications.'

'But she let them down. And you?'

'Made up for it.' He grinned self deprecatingly. I reckoned he was more perceptive than his nervous manner belied.

'I did computer sciences back when it was a new field. Had my own business for a while but now I work on a consultancy basis. Work on new programmes, look at IT packages for industry and commerce, do a bit of research as well – mainly artificial intelligence.'

His shyness evaporated as he talked work – he still avoided eye contact but there was a confidence in his voice and the emotional intensity in the atmosphere waned.

We talked a bit longer and he arranged to come back in two days time with as many starting points as he could find. He mentioned a neighbour he thought would be happy to help him recall the names of Jennifer's friends.

I'd already outlined my fees to him and we agreed that I would do the equivalent of three days work and then report back to him. At that stage he could decide whether to retain me.

It was almost lunch time and my stomach had begun to growl but I decided to complete my notes at the office before walking home. Office may give the wrong impression; it's a room in a cellar that I rent from a family who live nearby. When I first set up shop as a private investigator I knew commercially rented accommodation was way beyond my means. But Withington, where I live, has a mix of houses and as well as the council estate, the terraced rows and the estate of Hartley semis there are quite a few big Victorian and Edwardian semis like the one we live in. I thought someone might have a spare room going so I went door-knocking in the neighbourhood and the Dobson's were happy to give me a try. Several years on I'm still there, the detective in the cellar. The rent's unchanged and apart from the time when some suspects on a case of mine trashed the place it's been a trouble free arrangement.

I read through everything I'd written during my meeting with Roger. I had a much clearer view of his parents than I did of his sister. Only to be expected. He'd been eight when she'd left home – his memories would be little more than a series of snapshots, particularly as he'd not have had the opportunity to share anecdotes and stories of her with the family in the intervening years.

Working a missing person's case I like to build up a picture of the person; a feel for them. A character sketch to accompany the facts and figures. Their interests, likes and dislikes can be just as significant in determining where to look as their last reported sighting or hair colour. I once had to trace a man who had a passion for breeding fancy mice. His wife told me all about the new strain he had developed. On the strength of that I managed to track him down to Wolverhampton where he was living bigamously with a second spouse and was prominent in the fancy mouse community. He'd changed his name, moved town and severed his roots but he couldn't give up his obsession and it was his downfall.

I opened a new file, labelled it and enclosed my notes. I didn't intend to do anymore until Roger returned with the list of friends and acquaintances.

I must admit my first feelings about the case weren't all that hopeful. Jennifer Pickering had been gone twenty three years. The trail would be cold as stone. She'd been estranged from the family for longer than she'd been part of it. If there really had been no contact in all those years then somewhere along the line Jennifer must have decided to stay lost: not to attempt a reconciliation, not to try building bridges. She'd cut her losses and got on with a new life and I couldn't imagine she'd be all that pleased to be invited to her mother's death-bed. Especially as her mother didn't want her there.

I couldn't second-guess her reactions to her brother's desire for a reunion and her share of the inheritance. Pleasure, I'd hope. But people act in strange ways: guilt, regret or bitterness skewing their responses. It was all speculation anyway. I had to find her yet. And deep down, in my bones, I didn't think I would.

Chapter Two

I walked home briskly. My cheeks were glowing from the crisp bite in the air. It was a sharp, sunny autumn day. The distant sky was a dark, moody blue heralding rain and contrasting perfectly with the sand, copper and ruby coloured leaves.

Our house is a big Victorian semi in the south of the city. Manchester is a large sprawling conurbation, laying on the plain between the Pennine foothills to the north and the rich Cheshire farmlands to the south. Its history as a centre of trade, industry and commerce brought successive waves of immigrants to live and work here. Manchester was now home to a myriad of cultures. There are large, long established communities from the Caribbean, from India, from Bangladesh and Pakistan, from China and Ireland.

The city is cross-hatched by the old canals and railways that transported the goods back in the days of the industrial revolution. The Manchester ship canal provided a thoroughfare to bring cargo all the way from the coast to the docks. In Manchester they would meet each day to set the price of cotton for the world. Whoever first lived in our house probably made his money in that trade.

I made myself a cheese and pickle sandwich and a mug of tea. Sat to eat at the big kitchen table. The house was quiet: kids at school, Ray at college, Sheila, our lodger, at the library working on her project for university.

Ray was in love. I should have been pleased for him but I was anxious. If it became serious he and his son Tom might move out. They might decide to buy a place instead of renting. Ray and I had set up home together for mutual convenience. Two single parents, a child apiece, a big house we could rent indefinitely. He'd answered my advert, and we'd given it a trial. It worked. It worked really well. My daughter Maddie had a surrogate brother in Tom and Ray and I benefited from sharing out the relentless routine of childcare and chores. We'd become a family of sorts. If Ray and Tom went I'd have to try and replace them – and they felt irreplaceable. It would be such a wrench. Or maybe Laura would move in? Could that work? Would she want to move into a set-up like ours? It was hard to share a house, hard enough for families and for couples but for people who hadn't got those roles allocated there was so much to negotiate. Ray and I had done hours of that along the way. And we'd had our very own lodger from hell, too, as well as some people who just didn't want to share a home with others in the long run.

I recalled the pokey bedsit I'd been in with Maddie before we'd got the house, no bath, no garden. It felt like a trap, a punishment, never a sanctuary. What if Ray did move out and I couldn't find anyone suitable to share? We'd have to move too – I couldn't cover the rent. I didn't want to leave Withington, I liked it. It was handy for the library and the baths, there were enough shops to suit us, and a park, even a cinema. The hospitals in the area and the universities down the road provided employment and brought students into the mix of people who lived in the neighbourhood. I'd hate to move.

I sighed, cleared away my plate and went out into the garden, the big beautiful garden, and launched myself into activity. There were still flowers on the sweet peas even though the foliage was powdery with mould. I picked a handful and there were enough buds to leave the plants for another few days. I cut back the worst of the dead perennials, leaving the ornamental grasses, the mint and honesty for the frost to decorate. I piled the twigs up for a bonfire. There were two clumps of Michaelmas daisies still blooming, their puce flowers vibrant against the wall. I picked an armful. Gaudy, cheerful. I put them in a vase on the kitchen table.

The dark sky had passed over, holding onto its rain. I set off for school. Someone else had been busy: I could smell woodsmoke. Strictly not allowed – we live in a smoke free zone. I know bonfires are supposed to be terrible for the air but a bonfire once or twice a year is so good for the soul.

Maddie; my daughter, and Tom; Ray's son, are like chalk and cheese. Maddie, aged six, is sensitive, imaginative and fearful of all sorts of things. She's also temperamental, but I would think that because being her mother means I'm on the receiving end when she throws a wobbler. Tom, aged five, is fearless, he hurls himself at the world and remains on an even keel much of the time. His grandmother, who is known as Nana 'Tello, short for Costello, is Italian and both Ray and Tom have inherited an olive skin and glossy dark curls from her. Maddie, by contrast, is pale-skinned and has light brown hair. They squabbled lightly most of the way home and collapsed in front of the television when we got in. I started cooking tea for the three of us. Ray would be late back and Sheila, who rents our attic flat, caters for herself.

Half-an-hour later we sat down to veggie-sausages, mashed potatoes and broccoli. Broccoli is just about the only green vegetable that both Tom and Maddie eat. It seems to have something to do with its resemblance to a tree, or to lots of little trees

28

if you separate the florets. Maddie was constructing a forested landscape when she dropped one of her sausages. Digger the dog, sentinel beneath the table, snapped it up. Tom chortled. Maddie tried to be philosophical. 'I'm not bothered, I've gone off those sausages. They're horrible.'

'Can I have that one, then?' said Tom.

'No.'

'You said you've gone off them.'

They bickered on until I intervened. 'When Maddie's finished, if she doesn't eat her sausage, you can have it.'

Tom smiled. 'Goody.'

Maddie wolfed down the sausage.

As I washed up I thought about the new case. Mrs Pickering was dying and facing death might soften her attitude to her long-lost daughter. It was possible that Roger was exaggerating the animosity, though he said she'd bitten his head off then wept when he'd raised the question a year ago. Would Mrs Pickering be as unapproachable a year on?

I wondered whether she had ever heard from Jennifer; letters that she tucked away or tore up? Would she have shown them to her husband? If he was so strict perhaps she'd kept them from him. She had called Jennifer a disgrace. I tried to imagine feeling that way about Maddie. Not wanting to speak her name, ignoring her existence. I could picture myself being hurt or angry at things she might do but I couldn't envisage a situation where I'd turn my back on her. No matter what she'd done.

It could have worked the other way; and been Jennifer who had severed the tie. Hurt by their lack of support she may have decided to cut them off. Deny them the chance to relent or make amends. Had she been pregnant? If that had been the case wouldn't the Pickerings have wanted to see their only grandchild, once they'd got used to the idea? Or would their church regard the baby as unwelcome evidence of sinful behaviour? A burden of shame not a bundle of joy. Were they that harsh? By the seventies public attitudes to illegitimacy had relaxed a lot, but the church and its members may well have opposed such changes and clung doggedly to maintaining their own high standards in the face of moral decline and corruption.

I had a rush of memory. I had announced my pregnancy at the tax office where I was working. I was happy about it even though the pregnancy was unplanned. I joked about the struggle ahead being a single parent (oh, how little did I know) and accepted people's congratulations.

One young woman, a fundamental Christian, cornered me later. 'Sal, have you really thought about what you're doing?'

I was too shocked at her audacity to stop her before she launched into a speech about children needing fathers, and how there were places that could support someone in my position until I had the baby. When she got to the part about how many couples desperately wanted a baby and couldn't have one, I turned on my heels and walked away. I was shaking and horrified to find myself so upset. I blamed it on my hormones. I was also angry that I hadn't challenged her opinions on the spot and my mind went round and round working out succinct arguments and powerful statements that I should have flung back at her.

In the intervening years there had been occasional echoes of that disapproval from people I'd met and now and again the tabloid press or the government of the day would start demonising single-parents for reasons best known to themselves. How much worse might it have been for Jennifer two decades earlier?

Had she had the baby? Had she kept it? So many possibilities. I could feel my curiosity intensifying. I smiled to myself as I wiped down the sink. Some cases draw you in: others, I do well, competently, professionally but they don't reach out in the same way. Already I was intrigued by Jennifer Pickering. I wanted to know her story. If I could unravel it there would be personal satisfaction along with the sense of a job well done. I couldn't wait to hear from Roger Pickering. I was hooked.

He came with a printed list of names, addresses, phone numbers and notes. His initial awkwardness evaporated as we began working through the list. Two of the people were neighbours; Mrs Clerkenwell, who still lived in the adjoining semi, 'she always had dogs, we used to walk them', and Mr and Mrs Shuttle who had lived at the other side and had moved away, to Bradford. He didn't have a forwarding address for them.

'I've not had a chance to check if they are still in Bradford,' he said, 'I don't know if they'll be able to tell you very much but they knew her as well as any of the other neighbours.'

There were three friends listed. 'Lisa Monroe, she lived at the old vicarage on the corner and her parents are still there. They gave me this number for her in Chester. She's Lisa MacNeice now. The other two, Caroline Cunningham and Frances Delaney, the Monroes told me their names. Frances Delaney they think she's still in Manchester but they don't know where Caroline is now, Lisa might.'

'Do you remember them?'

'Vaguely, more as a gang than individually. Like I said they didn't come round to our house very often. But I think I was at school with one of Caroline's brothers, there was a Mick Cunningham in my year.'

Roger had added the number of Jennifer's old school. Had the girls been at school together?

'Not Frances, she went to the Catholic school – St Anne's.'

He'd brought a photograph of Jennifer as well. All dressed up to go out by the look of it; purple maxi skirt, black skinny rib sweater. She had long brown hair, parted in the centre, it gave her a sleek look. She was smiling. I studied her face; it was quite delicate, thin nose, small mouth, her eyes seemed large but that could have been the effect of the dark make-up. I tried to imagine how she would look now she'd aged twenty odd years. Difficult. So much would depend on how she dressed, how she wore her hair, if she wore glasses, jewellery, make-up.

Roger cleared his throat, 'Could you get this copied? There aren't many decent photos of her.' He shrugged, a little embarrassed, 'well, this is the only one I've got.'

'Yes, I can get some photocopies done, give you it back next time we meet.'

I told him I would be in touch after talking to some of the people on the list and let him know what progress I'd made.

After I'd seen him out I made myself a cup of coffee and then got busy on the phone. Mrs Clerkenwell could see me that same afternoon.

There was an answer machine on at Lisa MacNeice's. I asked her to return my call without going into any details.

Roger hadn't given me a number for the other neighbours; the Shuttles. However I did find a number for them – when I'd set up the business I'd invested in phone directories for the main northern cities as I expected at times my cases would take me to Leeds or Liverpool and they'd be useful resources. I checked the phone book for Bradford and found just one Shuttle. Felt like my lucky day (though I couldn't be dead certain it was the same couple). I wrote the number and address in my notebook for future reference. As they were no longer in the area and had moved away years ago I decided to wait before following them up. Jennifer's friends were much more likely to have heard from her.

I got a call then from Mandy Bellows at the Neighbour Nuisance Unit at Manchester City Council. I'd done a bit of surveillance work for them the previous year, helping to gather evidence that they could use to take an anti-social tenant to court.

'Sal, how are you?'

'Fine, and you?'

'Too busy, half the team's off ill with some nasty little virus and the rest of us are holding the fort. The reason I rang you,' she continued, 'I've some clients suffering harassment, general unpleasantness from the neighbours. I want to see if we can gather enough firm evidence to go to court. Can you pop in on Thursday to talk about it?'

'Yes, morning?'

'Good, ten o'clock?'

'Yes, see you then.'

More work, more money. It was rare that I was only working on one case at a time and when I did there were gaps in my working day while I waited to interview people or receive replies to enquiries made. It was much better when I'd a few things on the go at once and it also meant I was nearer to making a decent living out of the job. (Not good, just decent as in free of debts). It was a state I aspired to and achieved now and again, but never for long.

I glanced at the clock. There was just time to make a note of the areas I wanted to cover with Mrs Clerkenwell and pop home for a sandwich before our appointment. I was looking forward to finding out some more about Jennifer Pickering. I didn't expect any hot tips as to where she was now but I hoped to learn a little about how she had been back then; a young girl about to fly the nest. What had she been expecting when she'd left for university? Was she anxious about it or eager? Had the Pickerings ever confided in Mrs Clerkenwell about what Jennifer had done or whether she had been in touch? I had no shortage of questions. I hoped that she would be able to answer at least some of them.

Chapter Three

Heaton Mersey, the district where the Pickerings lived, isn't far from Withington so I made the journey on my bicycle. That and swimming are the only regular exercise I get. Now and again I practise sprinting as a very useful skill for a private investigator to possess but I'm afraid I don't do it as often as I should. Still I guess I could do a reasonable dash in the Mum's 100 metres at school's sports day – if they had a sports day.

The houses were good sized Edwardian semis, brick built, with tall, bay windows and sizable front gardens. Each had a driveway and garage. The gardens were well-tended. The neighbourhood looked settled, comfortable. Several windows sported Home Watch stickers.

I rang the bell for Mrs Clerkenwell and there was a burst of barking from inside. While I waited I looked at the adjoining house hoping to catch a glimpse of Mrs Pickering. There were no signs of life.

Mrs Clerkenwell opened her door. I introduced myself.

'Come in, I've shut the dogs in the garden, they get delirious over new people. Bring your bike in.'

'I can leave it in the back if you'd rather.'

'No problem. Can you manage?'

I wheeled the bike up the two steps to the front door and into the hall. There was plenty of space. I leant it against the wall, taking care not to scuff the wallpaper. We went along the hall to the back room and sat at a table by the window looking out onto the back garden. The rooms had high ceilings with moulded plaster edges and picture rails around the walls. It was decorated in creamy yellow with a mossy green for the woodwork. The colours lightened the room which could easily have been gloomy.

'Would you like a drink? Tea, coffee?'

'Coffee please, no sugar.'

She was a large-boned woman, in her fifties at a guess with grey shoulder length hair; a sallow complexion and chunky black-framed glasses. She wore dark slacks and a baggy woollen sweater, bottle green with flecks of colour in it, sprinkled with dog hairs.

From the chair I could see the garden, long and wide with a couple of apple trees at one side and a wall at the end. Flower borders ran the length of the lawn which had a wavy path down its centre. Two honey coloured Labradors were sniffing around the lawn and occasionally diving onto each other. An old larch-lap fence divided the garden from its neighbours on either side. I stood up to see what was visible of the Pickering's garden to the left. I could make out the roof of a garden shed and circular clothes dryer, the tips of a row of conifers at the far side, nothing more.

Mrs Clerkenwell returned with mugs of coffee.

'Roger has explained to you why I'm here? That he's asked me to trace his sister, Jennifer?'

'Yes. Though I'm not sure what help I'll be. I've often wondered what became of her.'

'What was she like?' I asked.

'Very lively, high spirits. Obviously got on well at school. Very bright, on the ball. She and Roger used to walk the dogs, he was not much more than a toddler when they first started. They'd take them down to the recreation ground or up to the park. Along the river sometimes. Once or twice she came along with me to a craft fair, I run a stall on a regular basis. She was a nice girl, I liked her.'

'And then she left home?'

'Yes, Keele wasn't it? English degree. Couldn't wait to get there. It was that terrifically hot summer, the drought. '76. You remember?'

I nodded. 'And after that?'

'I never heard from her. Not that I expected to. I was only the next-door neighbour,' she laughed.

'Did you know that she'd not kept in touch with her family?'

'Not for some time, no. I think it was that Christmas, I saw Barbara and I asked her about Jennifer; how she was getting on, when would she be back – that sort of thing. She was quite abrupt. Told me that Jennifer had dropped out of university and that they'd no idea when they would hear from her again. I was surprised, I must admit. I never thought Jennifer would have given up her studies like that. Perhaps the course wasn't what she'd expected. Anyway, Barbara obviously didn't want to talk about it and we were never very chummy so that was it.' She wrinkled her nose and the heavy glasses bobbed up and down.

I took a swig of my coffee, it was cool enough to swallow.

'When Frank died I thought Jennifer might be back for the funeral but she wasn't. It's not the sort of thing you can ask about really, though people noticed. So, I knew she'd not been back to visit but I hadn't realised that there had been no word at all until Roger called the other day.'

Mrs Clerkenwell had made no mention of a possible pregnancy, presumably Barbara Pickering had not referred to the disgrace her daughter had brought on the family as she had when talking to her son.

'Don't you think it's a bit extreme,' I asked her, 'to sever all contact, just because she dropped out of university?'

'Well, yes,' she said hesitantly, 'but then Barbara gave me the impression that it was Jennifer's doing.' She frowned and thought for a minute. 'Mind you, I don't know what sort of reception she'd have got if she had come back and wasn't making anything of her life.'

'How do you mean?'

'Well, they were awfully strict. Some of it was to do with all their rules, from their church, the do's and don'ts. They wouldn't touch a drink and everything was either approved or denied. I could see Jennifer was rejecting all that even before she left home. They were very ... intolerant I thought. We had a bit of a run-in years back. I was trying to organise some ecumenical services, different churches coming together and I knew Barbara and Frank were 'Children of Christ' but they were impossible; they'd no interest in building bridges, you'd have thought I'd made an improper suggestion the way they reacted. He started going on about undesirables and riff-raff and how could they vet the people involved.' She laughed. 'I don't know. I never knew them well but it didn't strike me as a very happy household.'

'Were there arguments?'

'Not between Frank and Barbara I don't think, but sometimes I'd hear Jennifer shouting at her mother – teenage tantrums I suppose. And Frank would lay the law down every so often. I'd hear him shouting some-times. He was very old-fashioned, all king and country. To be honest I think having Jennifer was probably completely bewilder-ing for him.'

'So you think it was Jennifer who made the break?'

'From what I was told. And it didn't sound as though they had done anything about finding her, I suppose they thought she was old enough to look after herself. And Frank was very ill, you know, that wasn't long after.'

'What was it?'

I drained my cup and continued to make notes.

'Angina. He stopped doing the garden. That used to be his pride and joy. We'd have a word over the fence. He struggled so hard during that summer with it, we couldn't use hosepipes, you know, everything was so dry but Frank was determined to make it work. Then suddenly he had to leave it all. I could see everything going to seed. Heartbreaking really. He got very low, depression. I never heard that from them, you understand, but word gets out. I don't think he ever really got better. It can take people like that can't it, sudden illness, they have to give up work and they never really find their way again.' She glanced out of the window and snorted. 'Look at that daft dog,' there was nothing but affection in her voice, 'excuse me a minute.'

She went out and into the garden where I watched her remove the hosepipe from the dogs' mouths thus curtailing their tug of war. I took the chance to glance back at the list of questions I'd come with. When she returned I began again.

'There's just a few more points.'

'Fine, it's a break from work,' she tilted her head towards the front of the house, 'there's a pile of stuff waiting in there for me to finish. I've got a big fair in Mobberley at the weekend. I'll show you before you go.'

'Yes. You were able to remember some of Jennifer's friends – Lisa and Frances and Caroline.'

'Fluke, really, though I am good with names. I know Frances Delaney and her family from church – St Winifred's. And it so happens that I used to give all four of the girls a lift up to the Bounty, it's closed now but back then it had banqueting suites and they were waitresses. I was doing table decorations there for a while but I had to let it go. It didn't really pay enough and it meant me missing some of the craft fairs. Anyway, the girls would come here and I'd give them a lift up on the Saturday morning, they'd share a taxi back or get a bus into town and another one out again.'

'Were you aware of any boyfriends at the time?'

44

'No, well nothing serious. Of course there was endless speculating and giggling but I was never privy to any secrets. I was just the next door neighbour with a car. Now I don't know if Frances still hears from Jennifer, have you got her number?'

I shook my head.

'Right,' she stood up and crossed to the table by the sofa, picked up the phone. 'She's not far away,' she said as she pressed the buttons, 'she's in Burnage. Lovely girl, four kiddies. Mary?' she spoke into the phone, 'it's Norma Clerkenwell … I'm fine … you? Listen, I've someone with me who wants to get in touch with Jennifer Pickering, from next door to me, does your Frances ever hear from her now? No. She's not said anything. Well, apparently they haven't, not in all this time. I'd Roger here the other day and he says they've no address or anything. It is a shame, it is … yes, especially with Barbara so poorly. Look, can you give me Frances' number and this lady might want to ask her a few questions – trying to trace Jennifer, you see. Great.' She wrote the number down on a pad by the phone. 'Thank you Mary, bye for now … and you, bye bye.'

She tore off the paper and gave me it.

'Mary says Frances has never mentioned Jennifer. That's her number. She's still Frances Delaney, married a boy with the same name.'

On the way out she opened the door to the front room to show me her wares. She'd put a large work table in the centre of the room and it was scattered with clumps of fabric, jam jars full of paint, trays with beads and coloured glass nuggets, small mirrors and assorted picture frames. Tools and brushes were stuck into a collection of vases in the centre. There was a smell of glue and varnish.

'Looks like chaos doesn't it,' she joked, 'you can see the finished results over there.'

The far wall was smothered with an array of fancy picture frames and mirrors, everything from tiny, stylish mosaic-edged mirrors to padded, frilled and be-ribboned portrait frames. There were plaques too, painted with house names and numbers and, at waist height, a long shelf held vases and jars decorated with vibrant glass mosaics.

'They're great,' I pointed to the vases, 'I love the mosaics.'

'They're selling like hot cakes at the moment,' she admitted. She edged her way past the table and picked up a small urn-shaped vase. 'Here,' she held it out, 'do you like this one?'

'Oh, no,' I protested, 'I can't.'

'It's good PR,' she insisted, 'when your friends admire it you can tell them where you got it. Word gets round, it all helps the business.'

'Thank you, it's lovely. You manage to make a living out of it?'

I thought of my friend Diane, a textile artist and printer whose income went up and down like a yo-yo.

'Now, I do. I'll just wrap this.' She pushed back her long, grey hair and rummaged in a carrier bag for some bubble wrap. 'The first few years were very hard. I made a loss for the first three. But I've a couple of big contracts with gift shops – that gives me a fairly regular return and the craft fairs and commissions top it up.' She tore some Sellotape from a dispenser and stuck it round the bubble wrap. 'There.'

'Thank you, it's lovely.'

'And I'll give you one of these,' she took a business card from a box on the table. 'I do orders to design, too.'

'Swap you,' I fished one of my cards from my pocket.

She helped me to manoeuvre my bike out of the door and down the steps to the path. She wished me luck with my search for Jennifer. 'I do hope you find her,' she said, 'I'd love to know how she's turned out, I always thought she'd make something of herself, you know.'

I couldn't make up my mind whether to keep the mosaic vase at the office or take it home where I'd see more of it. I dithered for a while. It looked great on the filing cabinet next to the cactus and the yucca, the tiny deep blue, turquoise and orange tiles complemented the colours in the room but not many of Mrs Clerkenwell's potential customers would see it there. I would leave it at work until I'd finished the job for Roger Pickering, a sort of talisman for the case. Then, whatever the outcome, I'd take it home and show it off.

I rang the number for Frances Delaney but there was no reply. I glanced at the clock. She'd probably be doing the school run. It was that time already.

Chapter Four

Lisa MacNeice rang me that evening. She sounded very cautious. Probably thought I was trying to flog her a new kitchen or a conservatory.

'I'm a private detective,' I explained, 'I'm trying to trace Jennifer Pickering on behalf of her family and I'd like to come and talk to you if I may.'

'Jennifer! Is this a wind-up? What's your name again?'

I told her. 'You can check with Roger Pickering if you like,' I said, 'he's still living at home.'

She reeled off the Heaton Mersey number. 'I can remember it after all this time. It's OK,' she continued, 'the private detective lark sounded a bit weird and I had some unwelcome attention from the press last year, dishing the dirt, you know. I thought it might be more of the same.'

'No, it's not.' I was intrigued; what dirt had been dished? I was dying to ask but I bit my tongue. 'In fact Roger's been to see your parents. That's how I got your number in the first place – you can confirm it with them if that would help.'

'No, it's OK,' she said, 'if you had been the press I'd be able to hear you squirming by now, spinning some yarn, either that or you'd have hung up. So you're looking for Jenny, I haven't see her since I left home, I've no idea where she is now.'

Oh no. I was disappointed. I'd been hoping for a break, wanting to hear that Jennifer had kept in touch with her friend and that Lisa could give me her phone number and address. Just like that.

'I realise it's a long time ago,' I said, 'but as yet I've no recent sightings to follow up. I'm having to go way back. When is the best time for you, if I were to come over?'

'Evenings, I'm usually home by seven.'

'Eight o'clock,' I suggested, 'tomorrow or the day after?'

'Tomorrow, yes.'

She gave me directions from the motorway and we said our goodbyes.

I was burning with curiosity about her references to the press? Perhaps I'd hear more about it when I met her. Or I could trawl around the news sites on the Internet, Ray was online now and I was having fun and getting frustrated at what I could and couldn't glean from it. If all else failed my friend Harry who was an investigative journalist turned Internet whizzkid would help out. He got a kick doing that sort of thing for friends, said it was light relief.

It occurred to me that I could search for Jennifer Pickering on the Net too. If she had e-mail it could be quite easy to find her address. It was too late in the day to try it now, I always spent twice as long staring at the screen as I'd anticipated, but I made a mental note to give it a go the next day.

I went down to the cellar to ask Ray if he'd be in the following evening – he hadn't mentioned anything but his relationship with Laura involved plenty of last minute arrangements. He had headphones on while he worked, he was varnishing a cherry wood corner cupboard. He'd used fretwork for the doors and it looked beautiful, intricate like lace.

'Ray.'

He straightened up and slid his headphones down.

'I have to work tomorrow night, someone I need to interview, I'll be leaving about 7.15.'

He nodded. 'I'll be here.'

'I shouldn't be too late back. That's looking good.'

'Bugger to varnish.'

I waited a beat or two sensing a slight awkwardness in the exchange. Nothing obvious. Symptomatic of how things had felt to me since Ray and Laura got involved with each other. He was always preoccupied. As if the rest of us had become minor supporting characters, there in the background but taken for granted. We definitely spent less time together and talked less. The worst thing was not being able to work out if my observations about the atmosphere were objective or if it was just my perception. It bugged me, it bugged me a lot.

Things were bound to change with a serious relationship, I kept telling myself, new lovers were notoriously selfish, maybe I was jealous (of Ray or of what they had?) Come on! I'd talk to Diane about it, my best friend, my confidante. She wouldn't shy away from being honest with me.

Thursday morning and I had an appointment with Mandy Bellows at the Town Hall. Withington is about four miles south of the City Centre and Wilmslow Road links the two in a straight line but I don't like doing that journey by bike so I got the bus in. That stretch has the dubious reputation of being the busiest bus route in Europe and although there are cycle lanes for part of it they are often used as handy parking spaces by motorists. You end up weaving in and out of aggressive traffic and waiting for the inevitable moment when some nerd does a sharp left turn across your handlebars or opens their door into you. Painful.

The bus journey was complicated by the annual intake of new students who were clutching maps and trying to find their way about, trying to get on the right bus to the right site on the right campus. Manchester boasts three universities and a handful of colleges and the city's population leaps by thousands every autumn.

They were a feature at every bus stop. Thankfully our driver was helpful and courteous. He patiently pointed out where the bus would go, corrected people's mispronunciations and called out loudly when we reached the various buildings on Oxford Road.

After living in Manchester, Keele would have seemed small to Jennifer Pickering, manageable. I'd a notion it was one of the out-of-town campus universities like Lancaster. I wasn't even sure where it was, Midlands? Somewhere near Stoke perhaps.

If Jennifer had got pregnant she must have met someone fairly early in the term. It takes a few weeks to make sure and I knew that she'd left Keele and had broken off contact by the Christmas. If I could find any people who were students with her, maybe people who shared her accommodation and did English with her they would be pretty likely to know who the man involved was, a student or a lecturer? Secrets were hard to keep in the close environment of university life. I remember in my own case we seemed to know everything about who was screwing who, who was into drugs or had debts or got violent when drunk.

At the top of Oxford Road there were adverts for new apartments in the heart of the city. Some of them were selling for ludicrous prices. Manchester was the place to be. We had the best football team in the world (according to Ray) and had produced Oasis as well as Coronation Street. Time was people in Manchester felt overshadowed by the dominance of London; people moved south for the opportunity to develop. But these days Manchester was on a roll. The centre of the universe. A Manchester accent was an asset – chuck.

The bus swung round past Central Library with its domed roof and pillars and I got off when it stopped near Albert Square.

It was a mild, misty day, the air felt soft. The Gothic style Town Hall with its honey sandstone seemed to glow against the colours of the surrounding trees and the slate grey of the sky.

The Neighbour Nuisance Unit is upstairs but I had to report to the security desk on the ground floor and they rang for Mandy to come down and collect me. She led the way up the stone staircase, between marble pillars with vaulted ceilings, everything rich with intricate stone mouldings and carvings. She made us coffee before we settled at her desk in the corner of the open plan office. She picked up a file from the sea of paperwork that cluttered her desk and spilled over onto a side table as well.

'Mr Ibrahim and his family came here from Somalia in 98. Refugees. They had two children, now three. They managed to get asylum. They were in London originally then got moved up here. They were in homeless families accommodation for a while then we offered them a house in St Georges, in

Hulme. They moved the first week of July. Since then there have been a series of incidents; verbal abuse, graffiti daubed on the house, stones thrown at the house, children threatened. They've reported it to the Housing Office and the police have cautioned some of those responsible.'

'Kids?'

'Not all of them. There's a family on the Close who have a reputation for anti-social behaviour; the Brennans. Neighbours have made a number of complaints about them to the council already and some neighbours have been asked to keep a diary to record any incidents. We will be seeking a court injunction to get them to alter their behaviour but it's going to take some time. However, there's another family, the Whittakers, and they seem to be the ones who are particularly targeting the Ibrahims. We've not had prior complaints about the Whittakers though I believe Colin Whittaker is known to the police, he's a member of some neo-Nazi group, he's banned from football matches – that sort of scene. From what Mr Ibrahim tells me he wants them out and he's making no bones about it.

'Now we can see about re-housing the family but as you know we would prefer to tackle the issue of anti-social behaviour or racial harassment and deal with those responsible. For that we need firm evidence to enable the police to take those involved to court. That's where you come in. We can give you a camcorder and one of the neighbours is prepared to let us use one of his rooms for surveillance. He's told us a lot about what's actually going on. I think he'd do it for us himself if we asked him but we need a professional job doing. You'll have to sort out a cover story, visiting relative or some such.'

My stomach missed a step. Surveillance is a mixture of dull and dangerous. But under-cover work which I have done on occasion demands even more nerve and involves play-ing a part with enough aplomb to convince. Surveillance is covert; the main aim to observe without being noticed, ninety-nine percent of the time it's a bore. Undercover work is both overt and covert, it involves being seen and being believed, fitting in or getting found out. The adrenaline never lets up, it can be terrifying. It is never boring.

'You know I can't do twenty-four hours?'

'We can work round that. The harassment usually happens when Mr Ibrahim is at work, in the evening. He's got a job at a take-away in Chorlton.'

'So Mrs Ibrahim's on her own with the children then?'

'Yes. It's not Mrs Ibrahim though, they have a different custom for names, she keeps her father's names even though she's married. All Somalis have three names, the children will take two of their father's names and be given a name too. So even they won't be known as Ibrahim. It gets very complicated,' she smiled, 'well, it does for us as you can imagine but the Somalis know exactly what's what.' She checked the file. 'She's called Fatima Hassan Ahmed, so you can call her Mrs Ahmed or Fatima – that's her given name. Now, there have been incidents at the weekends too and they seem to be increasing in frequency. We'd like you to start with a night this weekend, his shift is six to two, you could cover that. I'm hoping you'll be able to get the general picture, maybe do another night if you need to. In addition to that I want you to be on call – we'll ask Mr Poole, that's the neighbour, to ring you if trouble starts. The Ibrahims don't have a phone. Mr Poole has called the police for help in the past though he doesn't want it broadcasting.'

'Do the Brennans and the Whittakers know?'

'Not sure, they may have their suspicions. However Mr Poole's got a great deal of respect in the area, used to run the local Tenants group until a couple of years ago. If they go up against him there'll be a lot of antagonism from other neighbours. He's not such an easy target.'

I thought about the role Mandy wanted me to play. 'I might be coming and going quite a bit and at odd times if I'm on call. I'll need some cover to allow for that.'

The pair of us began to invent possibilities.

'District nurse?'

I shook my head. 'Too risky, people might know who the nurses are and he'd have to play sick as well. If I was a relative why would I be at Mr Poole's? Job interviews?'

'Training course?'

'They usually do accommodation. What about clearing my mother's house out? Recent bereavement.'

'Why not stay there?'

'Sick aunt in hospital?'

'You could stay at her place,' she objected.

'No, she lives in a nursing home, but she's gone into hospital for an operation or tests. She's my mother's sister, I'm the closest living relative – I can't afford a B&B.'

There was a pause while we both considered any major flaws in this scenario. It sounded general enough to be plausible and I wouldn't have to wear a uniform or gen up on any particular skills or knowledge. I would adopt some basic disguise though. Hulme was only a couple of miles north of my home in Withington and it was possible that in the future I'd run into someone who knew me from Mr Poole's, or somebody who knew me would turn up unexpectedly in Hulme and blow my cover. It would be safer to preserve a different identity.

'That'll do,' I said, 'Mr Poole can be a relative on the other side of the family and I'm up from London.'

Mandy gave me Mr Poole's address and phone number and pulled out a portable camcorder, tapes and spare battery from her drawer. It was a very compact model – ideal for spying. She took it out of the case and showed me the basics. She assured me it would record even in poor lighting unlike most models. I felt a little thrill at the prospect of doing the job.

'The most effective evidence,' she said, 'is obviously where we can see who is doing what. Remember to always keep the date and timer on and, if you can, start with a general shot to establish the scene then use the zoom to pick out the faces of those present.'

'Just like they do in the movies,' I joked.

'If there's any violence or the threat of any violence, ring the police immediately.' She packed away the equipment. 'And keep me informed, it's a nasty case and I'd like to see it resolved as soon as possible.'

I felt a mixture of excitement and apprehension about the task I'd been set but I had no premonition of how devastating it was going to be.

Chapter Five

I made my way through town to a photocopy shop. They were still re-building the centre, three years after an IRA bomb had gutted the city. Boards sectioned off parts of Cross Street as construction continued on the new Marks and Spencer building. Traffic to and from Victoria Station had to go round by the Cathedral or up Shude Hill. I had three copies done of the photo of Jennifer Pickering and then I walked up to Piccadilly to catch the bus back.

There was more work going on around Piccadilly Gardens. Manchester was in a constant process of change. The flourishing music business and club culture had brought confidence and development to the area. The city was a major tourist destination now. I was standing within spitting distance of Chinatown with its magnificent Chinese arch and plethora of restaurants, of the thriving gay village, host to the largest gay Mardi Gras in Europe, of the huge Greater Manchester Exhibition Centre and the Bridgewater Hall home to the Halle orchestra. A short ride on the Metro Link would get me to Old Trafford cricket ground or Manchester United football club. Not that I'd ever been.

I spent the afternoon in the office, writing up notes and planning how I would use my time over the next few days. Roger Pickering had dropped off his letter for the powers that be at Keele and I wrote one of my own to go with it, outlining again that I wanted to have any forwarding address for Jennifer Pickering believed to have left her course in the autumn term 1976. If they didn't have a record of that I asked whether they could give me details of Jennifer's Halls of Residence address while she was at Keele?

And could they provide any contact details for students there at the same time who might be able to assist me? I thought the latter was a long shot really and my hopes were resting on them coming up with the address that Jennifer had moved to. Then I'd take it from there.

After a top-up of caffeine I rang and introduced myself to Mr Poole, thanked him for his offer, and asked if I could come to his house that Friday evening to start my surveillance.

'I'll pretend to be a distant relative,' I said, 'my aunt's in Wythenshawe hospital having tests and I'm visiting from London.'

'If anyone asks,' he said, 'I'll tell them you're one of Joan's children. My son Malcolm remarried and moved down south. Joan already had three children from her first marriage. You'd be a step-granddaughter, I reckon. You'd not be expected to know much about this side of the family.'

'That sounds great, and we needn't have met before. I'll use my own first name – Sal, Sal Smith will do.'

Mr Poole cleared his throat. 'What exactly will it involve? You being here.'

'I'll have a camcorder, a video, to record anything that goes off. I'll keep it running whenever there's any activity outside the Ibrahim's, so most of the time I'll be perched in the window filming or watching for something to happen. I hope to leave in the early hours when Mr Ibrahim is back from work. And if anything happens before then will you ring me on this number – have you got a pen?'

I gave him my number and the one for my mobile and said I'd see him Friday. He seemed to be taking the whole set-up in his stride and I was looking forward to meeting him, impressed at how he was prepared to get involved and resist the threat of violence that came with the territory.

I managed half an hour on Ray's computer searching for an e-mail address for Jennifer Pickering, J. Pickering, Jenny Pickering and J.L. Pickering.

I found three matches in all, two in the United Kingdom and one in Hawaii. I sent messages to all of them asking them to reply and confirm whether they were Jennifer Lesley Pickering formerly of Manchester, U.K. and giving her birthdate. I also left instructions for two search engines to carry on searching and give me the results later.

Of the UK matches there was a J. Pickering in London but that could have been a John or a Julie, and a Jennifer Pickering in Scarborough. This last one seemed to be the most likely – she'd given her full name but not bothered with her middle name. I tried not to get too excited about it but my imagination kept running scenes where I checked my e-mail and found a great big 'Yes, that's me!' message waiting for me. Oh, if only…

Chester is about thirty five miles south west of Manchester towards North Wales. I allowed myself three quarters of an hour to get there which was about right. When Maddie and I have holidays we often go camping in Wales, so the journey reminded me of setting off, desperately trying to remember exactly what I had forgotten to pack.

I played an old Gypsy Kings tape, yelling along to the rousing tunes and crooning to the lovesick ballads. It was a mild night and dark by the time I left the motorway and followed Lisa's directions. I only took one wrong turning and arrived outside her bungalow at five to eight. The windows were aglow and there was a car in the drive. The estate was open plan, no walls or hedges in the front gardens. Easier to see what the neighbours were up to. I wondered what effect it had on people's interaction. Did it increase a sense of community, everyone looking out for everyone else or did people draw away from each other, bothered by the lack of privacy?

I rang the bell and heard it sound inside the house, moments later Lisa MacNeice answered the door. 'Sal Kilkenny?'

'Yes,' I handed her my card which she actually looked at before pocketing it and inviting me in.

I could smell onions and the tang of herbs. There were rooms off to either side of the hallway but we passed these and went to the back where a kitchen cum dining room ran the width of the house.

'Do you mind?' she gestured to the plate on the table, 'I was just finishing off.'

'No, carry on.' Tagliatelli and pesto by the look of it, tomato and red onion salad. My mouth watered even though I'd had a decent meal already. I pulled out a chair, shrugged off my jacket and sat down. She ate while I admired the decor.

The room was bright, stylish and spacious. Blue kitchen units with that distressed paint finish ran along one wall and on the adjoining side next to the door stood a beautiful pine dresser resplendent with a collection of hens and chickens in all shapes and sizes. The rear wall was mainly French windows with sheer curtains. In the dining area there were shelving and storage units in wood and glass, holding books and objects of interest, many of these were blue or orange. A side table sported a large vase of lilies, I caught their perfume now that I'd got used to the smell of food, and a six foot Yucca stood sentinel in the corner.

'You collect chickens?' I remarked.

'I never meant to,' she swallowed, 'one of those things, I had a couple and then all of a sudden rumour flies round that I adore hens and that's all I get; birthdays, Christmas, the lot. "Ooh, there's a tea caddy with hens on, ooh look, Lisa would love that chicken letter opener".'

I laughed.

'Hard to shake once you get that sort of reputation. You wouldn't believe some of the ghastly specimens I've ended up with – these are the cream of the crop.' She rolled her eyes. She had very pale blue eyes, almost turquoise. She was small and neat, dark hair cut in an elfin shape to frame her face. When she smiled she had matching dimples in her cheeks. She wore deep blue chinos and a brushed cotton shirt in a blue and white check. I think she liked blue. Silver earrings and necklace, no rings. Divorced then?

She stood and cleared her plate and offered me a drink. I asked for a coffee and also if I could use her toilet.

'End of the hall, on your right.'

Other people's bathrooms. Fascinating. Lisa's had the feel of a beach hut, without the sand on the floor. Blue, pink and white striped shower curtain, white painted floorboards, shells and marine artefacts dotted about. An old wooden trunk to sit on. I peered on the shelves but there were no male toiletries, no Gillette foam or Lynx deodorant. I guessed that Lisa lived alone.

Over coffee I asked Lisa to tell me about the last time she saw Jennifer.

'It was that summer, '76. I got these out after you rang.' She fetched a photograph album from the shelves. I moved my chair round so we could look at the pictures together. She flicked through the first few pages and I caught glimpses of family scenes, babies and toddlers on rugs, school photos.

'Here,' she said, 'this was my 16th birthday.' The photo showed four young women, arms linked across shoulders, standing outside. They all had long hair and wore high boots, long coats and scarves, plenty of glittery make up. The glam rock look.

'That's Frances,' she pointed to the one with blonde hair, 'Frances Delaney, she didn't go to school with us but she lived near Jennifer, house at the back of theirs. Jenny,' looking sleek and dark haired, 'me, I was a right pudding then.' Her hair was thick and curly and it was true she was a plump teenager. The fourth girl, Caroline, had glasses and long red hair.

'Christmas that year,' she turned the page. More photos followed, all pretty similar, the girls posing for one celebration or another. Lisa and Jennifer pulling faces in one shot, the four of them posing with arms flung skywards in another. Clothes varying but hair always long, faces made up. There was a photo of them in waitress uniforms, the long tresses pulled back into ponytails and buns. 'That's at the Bounty, we worked there weekends, silver service, it was good money really. And we'd usually enough energy to go out and spend some of it after-wards.'

'I met Mrs Clerkenwell, she remembers giving you lifts up there.'

'Oh, yes,' I could hear a note of recollection in her voice, 'nearly quarter of a century,' she shook her head.

'Were you and Jennifer close?'

She looked at me, considering. 'Insepar-able,' she said at last, a tone to it though, a faint challenge? I couldn't read it.

'We were best friends. It was strange that summer. We were both off to university, so excited but there was this,' she fumbled for a word, 'sense of something coming to an end, I suppose. That sounds dramatic but we'd been so wrapped up in each other's lives I couldn't imagine how I'd feel without Jenny. Oh, we'd promised to write and visit each other for weekends, I think we even talked about trying to get jobs in the same place once we'd graduated, and sharing a flat,' she smiled and her dimples re-appeared, 'never any thought that we might lose touch.

'Anyway we were both working that summer, Jenny had got more hours at the Bounty and I was working in Kendal's in town.' She turned the page. 'When we got time off when went to Knebworth – bril-liant, Lynnryd Skynnyrd, 10cc, the Stones,' she pointed to a picture of the two girls beside a small, drooping tent, their hair was plaited and they had hearts and stars painted on their cheeks. 'Just look at us, and those trousers, flapping around like bedsheets, came back in fashion last year, skinny rib sweaters. God, when I think of what we got up to, we'd no fear,' she shook her head. 'That's when we saw Bob Marley. That was incredible – just after the Handsworth riots and everyone was saying Moss Side would be next, police everywhere – but it was fine.'

She looked across at me. 'She couldn't wait to leave home. Her parents,' she paused, swung her aquamarine gaze away from me, considered a while, 'looking back I just don't think they'd a clue about how to raise a family. There was no love or affection. They weren't cruel or anything – there was just this absence of any warmth. Jennifer and Roger were their duty, that's all. Of course they were very strict as well, religious and set in their ways. They hated the way Jenny dressed and all the make-up, they didn't like her going off to concerts and parties. They couldn't see she was just having fun, doing normal teenage things. I know at that age we all think our parents are the pits and I had a good few run-ins with mine but Jenny's were in a different league really. Her mother was so distant, quiet.

Maybe she was depressed. And her father was all stiff upper lip stuff, really formal. Very sad, really. I'm amazed Jenny was as sane as she was. You say Roger's still at home?'

'Yes.'

She shuddered. 'Poor bloke.' She closed the book. 'It was brilliant that summer and then,' she flicked her eyes at me as if weighing something up, she decided to tell, 'Jenny got pregnant.'

'That summer?' Not once she'd gone to Keele. 'Who was the father?'

She sighed impatiently, the memories irritating even at this distance. 'Maxwell, he was the sous-chef at the Bounty. She didn't know what to do. It wasn't part of the plan. We were so young. God, it was a nightmare. She was so confused. One minute she was talking about abortion – she reckoned she could use part of her grant to pay for it, or we'd scrape the money together and she'd pay us back once she got her grant through. Then she'd go all weepy and talk about the baby and deferring a year.' She tutted with exasperation.

'What did she do?'

'I don't know,' she stared at me, 'I never heard.' There was a bitter edge to her voice.

'One minute she's round my house every night going over it all and next thing she's left. I rang her up, Mrs Pickering answered, said she'd gone to Keele. It was another week till Fresher's week; I didn't know you could go early. Then I thought maybe she'd gone to get an abortion, have a few days to deal with it. I didn't know if she'd said anything to her parents, there wasn't really any point unless she went ahead and kept the baby and they'd have gone barmy, her Dad was a right bigot, he'd hardly be chuffed at a mixed race grandchild. But I had to ask, I was so embarrassed. I didn't want to drop her in it, I said something like "Has Jenny told you she's not been feeling all that well?" Talk about euphemisms. There was a pause, I can still remember that because I felt so awkward and I thought she was going to sound off at me but all she said was, "no, she's been fine," so I assume she hadn't told them.

'After that I got really cross. The little shit had gone off without a goodbye or anything. It wasn't my fault she'd got caught out but it felt like she was lumping me in with everyone else, wanting to leave us all behind. I called her all the names under the sun.

'Then I went off to Newcastle and I was so

73

busy that Jennifer didn't seem all that important anymore. But I didn't just leave it. I rang her family later that term to ask how she was getting on and to check her address – I'd written a note to the Halls of Residence at Keele but I never got a reply. Anyway her Mum said she'd left the course and they'd no idea where she was. I said maybe they should report her missing and she said "she's not missing, she's just being very silly, throwing it all away, we'll have to wait till she comes to her senses". She said she'd no idea why Jenny had jacked it in. I wondered if she was keeping the baby, but she didn't want to tell them yet or maybe she was going to have it adopted and felt that the less people that knew about it the better, sort of thing. But I was worried and I still couldn't understand why she hadn't written to me or phoned me, or left a message. Her parents, yes – but me, we'd been best friends.'

She turned the bracelets round on her wrist, worrying at them. 'I did actually go to the police you know, that first Christmas. I was back home, she wasn't, no card had come. I'd this vision of her six months pregnant, squatting in London or something. So I smartened myself up and went to the police station. They listened for a bit but when I said the family weren't particularly concerned they lost interest. They let me fill a form in but that was it. I didn't know half the answers anyway, I wasn't sure of her last address so I just put Halls of Residence Keele University, I didn't know when she'd last been seen or what she'd been wearing – all those things.'

'And she never wrote?'

She shook her head. 'I still don't understand that. I think,' she hesitated, her assurance slipping for a moment, 'I think maybe something happened to prevent her getting in touch.'

'What sort of thing?'

'An accident or ... if she ended up broke in London, the options for earning money aren't very safe, or problems with the baby ... I don't know, a breakdown?'

'You've mentioned London a couple of times, did she talk of going there?'

'Not particularly, Paris was our dream. London's just where people went to escape – still do I suppose.'

The big smoke, I thought, big enough to get lost in, stay lost in.

'If she had been hurt, if she'd died,' she spoke the unthinkable quickly, 'could you find that out?'

'If that had happened, her parents would have been informed,' I pointed out.

'But what if she'd changed her name or they couldn't identify her, something like that?'

'Then she wouldn't be on any records that I could find. There are General Records, you know, births, deaths and marriages but they won't record people who haven't been identified.'

'And she might be happily married and living in Crewe,' Lisa replied.

'Could be. If I don't get a lead I may well be able to check out the records for marriages as a way of tracing her but before that I'm talking to people who knew her and checking with the university. Can you think of anywhere else Jennifer might have gone after she left Keele, anyone she'd ask for help?'

'No.'

'And she never contacted any other friends?'

'Not that I heard. I haven't seen the others for a few years now.'

'Have you got a number for Caroline Cunningham?'

'Yes, if she's still there. Hang on.' She

moved across to the shelves and flicked through a large leather bound book. Found what she was looking for and gave me the number.

'What about Maxwell, do you think she ever got in touch with him?'

She raised her eyebrows. 'I doubt it. He's still around, has a fancy restaurant in Sale, The Grove – I only know because they reviewed it in the Guardian. He's done very well for himself.'

'Did Jennifer tell him she was pregnant?'

'No, it was awful, he'd broken it off just before she found out. He was playing the field, no intention of settling down. She wouldn't have married him anyway, he was, childish really, very self-centred. She'd enough on her plate without him as well.'

'What's his surname?'

'Jones, Maxwell Jones.'

I thanked Lisa and stood up. She picked up the photograph album and hugged it to her. 'I still dream about Jenny sometimes, even after all these years,' she shook her head as if that were a failing.

'If you think of anything else, you've got my card.'

'And if you find her, give her my number, I'd like to hear from her. I bet we'd get on just as well as ever.'

As she saw me out I realised Lisa had made no mention of the press attention that she'd alluded to on the phone. I felt it would be crass to ask her about it at that point. It wasn't any of my business. My business was to trace Jennifer Pickering and I wasn't exactly hot on the trail.

The journey home was straightforward. The towns and villages either side of the motorway were clusters of lights. The major roads defined by ribbons of light like strings of beads spilt across the black fields.

I didn't seem to be getting anywhere fast talking to Jennifer's old friends. OK I had established that she'd been pregnant but that brought me no nearer knowing how to contact her. I reckoned my best bet lay with anything that Keele University could tell me. I'd still go ahead and see the remaining people on my list, it wouldn't hurt to talk to them see if they could shed any more light on the mystery. She'd left home before the induction week at Keele, had she been to a clinic to have an abortion during that gap? Had she confided in any of her friends? Lisa claimed she and Jennifer were very close, if she'd not told Lisa would she have told Frances Delaney or Caroline Cunningham?

Could there be any other reason for leaving home sooner than expected? I rolled my shoulders back, becoming stiff from the driving, noticed my hands were gripping the wheel a touch too tight for comfort, I made an effort to relax them. I pushed a tape into the cassette player, Ladies of Jazz, sang along to the smouldering lyrics, let the smoky voices lead me home.

Chapter Six

The next morning was glorious. Sky like fresh paint, sun full of warmth. The sort of day for walking up hills, climbing on top of the world and marvelling. I made it to school, Tescos and the Health Food Shop in Withington. And spent most of the rest of it at the office connecting up with people who could tell me more about Jennifer Pickering circa 1976.

I got through to Caroline Cunningham who sounded to be lost in a heavy cold. I explained who I was, how I'd got her number and what I wanted to talk to her about.

'Honestly?' Her voice rose to a squeak.

'Yes, I'm talking to all her old friends and neighbours. Whereabouts are you?'

'Sheffield, are you coming from Manchester?' She began to cough.

I waited for her to stop before I replied and used the time to calculate whether I could make the journey there and back and be certain of being able to pick up Maddie and Tom. It was too tight, I didn't need to kill myself over a visit to Caroline. 'Yes, it would have to be Monday though, if you'd be at home.'

'Yes, there's no way I'm goid in like this,' she coughed again to prove her point, 'the doctor said take a week minimum. Bordig?'

It took me a second to translate. 'Morning would be fine. I'll aim to get to you about eleven.'

'OK.'

The phone was engaged at Frances Delaney's house. I put a cross on my list, I'd try her again later.

I made a coffee and had it with the vegetable samosas and the tomato that constituted lunch. I washed the grease off my hands upstairs; the Dobsons let me use their bathroom. The shelves bulged with bath-stuffs and cosmetics and towels were stuffed onto rails and hooks any old how. Four girls lived here and the array of bottles bore witness. I'd this to look forward to with Maddie – and teenage rebellion. I knew that the Dobsons had an easy time with their eldest – she was eager to travel and had been too busy earning cash for her adventure to be out clubbing it or in slumming around. It was different with their second girl. They were in the throes of teenage hell. The fact that both parents were teachers and had masses of experience working with youngsters hadn't seemed to help at all.

Jennifer had been a typical teenager, eager to become independent, desperate to leave home. Her parents had disliked her clothes and the lifestyle she enjoyed but didn't that just come with the territory? I was becoming more convinced that I would have to speak to Mrs Pickering eventually. If anyone could tell me the essential facts it had to be her: exactly when Jennifer had left her course at Keele, whether she'd given any indication whatsoever of where she was going, whether she talked about having a baby. After all at that point Mrs Pickering had deemed her daughter a disgrace. Hardly a term for someone who'd dropped out of an English degree. If I didn't get any joy from Keele I would have to persuade Roger to let me approach his mother.

The neighbours who had lived on the other side of the Pickerings had moved to Bradford. I dialled their number. 'Hello?'

'Is that Mrs Shuttle?'

'Yes.'

'You used to live in Heaton Mersey?'

'Yes.'

'My name's Sal Kilkenny,' I began, 'I'm trying to trace a missing person, Jennifer Pickering, I know you and your husband lived next door to the Pickerings while Jennifer was still at home.'

'I don't know anything about all that,' her voice was glacial, 'I can't help you.' She hung up on me.

I sat there for a moment stunned by her abrupt dismissal. I toyed with the notion of ringing her back to press the issue but I realised it would be a futile thing to do. The woman obviously didn't want to have anything to do with me. Why? It happens that people shut the door in my face. It happens quite a lot actually, especially when I'm serving injunctions. But in other cases there's generally a little more interaction before people choose not to get involved, not to answer questions, not to waste their time. The speed of her decision and the frostiness of her response got me thinking that there must be some history there, some reason for Mrs Shuttle to turn arctic at the mention of the Pickerings. It was the only untoward reaction I'd had and it intrigued me, made me want to start burrowing away to find out what lay behind it. Oh, it was probably something innocent like the two families had fallen out over a border dispute or the Shuttle's cat had persisted in fouling the Pickering's garden, maybe Jennifer had been a bit lippy to the neighbours. Whatever it was I didn't know whether it would bring me any closer to finding Jennifer and I wasn't sure that I should pursue it. I thought it was probably a red herring albeit an interesting one. I know better, now.

I finally got through to Frances Delaney and explained why I was calling.

'Can it wait till after the weekend?' she asked. 'It's just that I've had one of them off with chicken pox and my husband's parents are visiting, arriving tomorrow. I've not even done the shopping…'

'That's fine,' I interrupted. I didn't need any more persuasion. 'I've already got things booked for Monday, some time on Tuesday perhaps?'

'Erm… About ten thirty? The baby usually has a nap then and Gemma will be at play-group. How long will it take?'

'An hour at the most, probably less.'

'OK. I'll give you the address.'

I wrote it down and said goodbye. So I couldn't see either of Jennifer's remaining friends until the following week. I'd still a couple of hours until school finished and that evening I began my surveillance for the Ibrahims. I could usefully prepare for that.

Coming back from school we looked for conkers. There are two huge horse chestnut trees on the way. Tom charged around lamming bits of stick enthusiastically into the trees while Maddie systematically combed the area looking for conkers on the ground.

After ten minutes we had a reasonable haul and at home we set about conducting an experiment. Two conkers each went into vinegar to soak, two each in the oven to bake. We would see which turned out toughest. Meanwhile I took a handful down to the cellar where Ray has his woodwork shop and drilled holes in them. We threaded them on bits of string and bootlaces. Tom and I played the first game. Taking turns to bash each other's conker with our own. After half a dozen strikes my conker split in half much to Tom's delight. Seeing this Maddie decided she wanted to keep hers to look at 'not ruin them like that' and she took them up to her room to a place of safety. After one more match which Tom also won, he went to watch telly and I started making tea. While I peeled vegetables and boiled rice, my mind turned to work and I wondered what awaited me later that day. My stomach fluttered with anticipation and not the pleasant sort.

The area of St Georges where the Ibrahims lived had all the depressing features of urban poverty. Just one of the row of shops I passed remained open though only the illuminated sign gave the game away as the windows were covered with steel shutters and the roof edged with vicious looking razor wire. The surrounding shops were boarded up, and covered in graffiti. Litter pooled around the pavements and broken glass glimmered in among the weeds.

Several of the houses also had broken or boarded up windows and one was blackened by fire. A little further along a car had met the same fate, its charred shell yet to be removed by the authorities.

I turned into Canterbury Close and drove along looking for Mr Poole's. There were semi-detached, red-brick houses either side and a turning circle at the dead end. The road curved so it wasn't possible to see the junction once I reached his house which was about half way down on the right hand side. Most of the houses looked in need of repairs and a fresh coat of paint. The council had been selling off stock but this wasn't the sort of area where tenants would exercise their right to buy even if they had the means. All the houses had gardens and, here and there, I could see the proof of someone putting in time and attention: trees in autumn finery and winter pansies in a hanging basket. For others the garden was left untended, left for the children to run wild in or used to dump rubbish.

I parked outside Mr Poole's and looked across at the Ibrahim's. There were two rough rectangles of black paint daubed on the brickwork beneath the lounge window and on the door – presumably to cover up the graffiti left by their tormentors.

I picked up the sports bag which held the camcorder, my mobile phone and my handbag, got out of the car and locked it.

There was a group of youths at the bottom of the close, clustered round a motorbike. They cast glances my way, one of them made a comment and there was a shout of laughter from the others and a medley of obscenities. I wondered whether my disguise was inciting any more interest than I would have done without it. I'd limited it to a few basic features – glasses with bright red frames, red lipstick, a light-weight grey wig and a stone-coloured mac. The glasses and wig came courtesy of my friend Diane who has a thing about trying out a new look every week or two and who lets me use her cast-offs when she goes off them. I can't often use her clothes – Diane is a very big woman, she's several sizes larger than me and makes most of her own stuff as the shops don't cater to her size or her wacky tastes. The glasses were clear lenses (I ask you) so at least I could see through them without endangering anybody, the wig (grey? what possessed her to buy grey?) was light enough to bear wearing for a few hours without getting a headache though it did make me itch round the hairline and the coat was a bargain buy that I've never worn. I kept trying it on but it just wasn't me.

With this costume my hope was that

anyone who met me would only remember an older woman with red specs.

Mr Poole was a large, well-built man with a mane of silver-grey hair, jowelly cheeks, a bulbous nose. Behind tortoiseshell glasses I could see small brown eyes, above them eyebrows run wild. He wore dark trousers and shirt and an old-fashioned cable knit cardigan, the sort with leather buttons.

'Come in, come in,' he stood aside and waved me through. Once he'd shut the door he took a moment to look at me, made no comment on what he found then announced, 'I'll show you round, there's three windows look across the street. This one,' he took me into the front room, 'and two upstairs.'

'It's very good of you to let me use the place.'

'Well, someone's got to do something. It gets my goat, it really does, the way they behave. Barbaric. I'd say they was like animals but that would be an insult to the animals. Now, you can see through here.'

We moved into the bay window. I could see through the nets into the house opposite and it was a reasonable view but I was aware that this was Mr Poole's living room and I would be shooting in the dark to avoid discovery. I thought I'd be better upstairs, a better chance to scan the street with less disruption for him.

We looked upstairs. 'I don't use either of these,' he said, 'I sleep at the back, it's quieter. This is the bigger one,' he switched on the light and a jumble of cardboard boxes and furniture appeared. 'I use it for storage,' he said, 'mind you, I've no use for half this lot, keep meaning to have a clear out, get the Sally Army round to take it away but I never find the time.'

The smaller room had more of the same but the view was slightly obscured by a telegraph pole so I settled on the larger one.

'I'll close the curtains,' I said, 'while I get sorted out. Can I use one of these chairs? Thanks. And when I film I'll part the curtains but I'll have the lights off so I can't be seen.'

Mr Poole watched while I moved some of the stuff around until I could place the chair a couple of feet away from the window. I set up the tripod and fixed the camera on. I'd no need to hand hold it while I was filming from the one position. If I did need to move the camera there was a quick release button securing it to the tripod. I turned off the light then opened the curtains a few inches either side until I could pan right across from left to right without filming curtain. I could zoom in on the Ibrahims' house and pull back to incorporate houses on either side and much of the nearby street. I couldn't see the main road from here but the bottom end of the Close was visible and I could film there if I swung the camera right at an angle. I shot a few seconds than played it back in the camera to check everything was working alright.

'Probably be a couple of hours before anything gets going,' he said, 'Mr Brennan likes to get a few jars down him before he starts picking a fight.'

'Does he live on the Close?'

'At the end, him and Whittaker, they've the houses either side of the alley at the bottom. It's been hell up here these last couple of years.'

'They told me there've been a lot of complaints.'

'That's right. Even though most people are afraid to say anything – scared that there'll be comeback if they do. You can't blame them, especially the young ones with kiddies. Leastways I've only myself to worry about. Come on down I'll make you a cuppa tea.'

He pointed out the toilet and bathroom on the way downstairs, 'Help yourself, whenever you need.'

His kitchen had never been modernised and some of the items, like the fifties dresser with its sliding frosted glass doors, were collectors items now for those into retro and kitsch. He made the tea slowly, methodically and we took the drinks into the lounge.

'So how did you come to be doing this?' he asked. 'Private investigator.'

'Enterprise Allowance Scheme.'

He guffawed. 'I heard of people setting up painting and decorating that way and catering but they let you do that?'

'Oh, there were all sorts,' I said, 'a juggler and an interior designer. I think the strangest of my lot was a snake breeder.' I thought back to the training sessions; lectures on self-employment, VAT and tax. A motley group of us, out of work but full of schemes and dreams.

'You got money on top of your benefit?'

'Yeah. Forty quid a week for a year, then sink or swim. They reckoned two-thirds of us would sink.'

'You didn't.'

'Near thing sometimes though.'

'They don't have that now,' he said.

The steam from my tea misted my glasses, something I wasn't used to. I pulled back and they cleared. 'I can't keep track,' I said.

'Seems to be going the American way; welfare to work, cutting people's money if they won't take a job. I can't see as how it's going to make anything better, not round here. Folks aren't going to be any better off, doing a dead-end job for the same money as the dole, that's not going to change people's futures, is it?'

I shrugged, probably not. And there but for the grace of God...

'And what about these single parents?' He persisted. 'Some lasses round here have two and three kiddies, they're looking after them best as they can, and it's hard for some of them, I can tell you. And now the government wants them to go out to work and pay someone else to mind their children. They might want to mind them themselves. Ought to pay them to do it. That's what my wife used to say – raising a family is work and it ought to be accounted for.'

But meanwhile? I thought. I drank my tea. 'Some of them might want the chance to work,' I said.

'All power to them,' he said. 'But if we go

down the road of pushing people into jobs they don't want; that or starve. That's not what we set up the Welfare State for,' his voice shook and got louder, 'we wanted to protect the most vulnerable – for the good of us all. Create a strong society. Give people the basics, decent housing, decent food, healthcare when they need it, every-one paying in, everyone benefits. Common interest, if we lose sight of that...' He broke off, rubbed his face with his hands. 'I'm sorry,' he said, 'on my soapbox, hard habit to break.'

Shouting from outside startled both of us. I went and pulled aside the curtain. A crowd of youths were on the pavement, five of them. Two were leaning against my car. They were laughing and joking. Mr Poole joined me, he took off his glasses and screwed up his eyes.

'The two with ginger hair, on the car,' he said, 'they're Brennan's twins, can't tell 'em apart. I don't know the two in the middle and the lanky one on the right is Micky Whittaker.'

He had a shaved head and a pattern marked on his scalp. 'What's that on his head?'

'A tattoo, bulldog.'

'His father is mixed up with some neo Nazi group.'

'Yes and his father gave his life fighting the fascists. Died in Malaya, and now sonny boy's running round celebrating Hitler's birthday.' Contempt riddled his voice.

'I'd better get them off the car,' I said. I pulled my coat back on and Mr Poole followed me to the door. I opened it and called. 'Can you get off the car, please.'

Jeers catcalls. One of the twins mimicked me, 'Can you get off the car, please,' and the other echoed him.

'Needs scrapping,' Micky Whittaker kicked a tyre with his boot. 'We can do it for yer, you'll get the insurance.'

I resisted joining in the banter and repeated my request.

'We're not hurting it,' said one of the twins, 'are we?' he turned to the others.

'No,' they chorused.

'Get off the car.'

'Alright, alright,' said the other twin.

'She's shitting herself,' one of them sniggered.

My cheeks burned but I tried not react.

'Come on, lads,' Mr Poole's voice was hard but not threatening.

'Alright, grandad, who's yer visitor?'

He took a step down and went to the gate. 'She's my niece, up from London and her auntie is poorly in the hospital so I'd appreciate a bit of peace and quiet while she's staying here, OK?'

There were shuffles and sniggers and a soft ''kin 'ell' from one of them as they shambled off down the road.

Chapter Seven

Half an hour later the motorbike I'd seen on arriving became the focus for some excitement. The driver roared it up and down the Close screeching to a halt at the bottom where the gang had congregated.

I told Mr Poole that I'd film some of this for the record.

'If you need anything,' he said, 'just give us a yell. I'll be in the back room,' he gestured in that direction.

'What time do you go to bed?' I felt slightly foolish asking but I didn't want to disturb him.

'Oh, I'll be up till you're done.'

'Are you sure, it'll be after two?'

'I only need a couple of hours these days,' he said, 'don't worry about me.'

I went upstairs and shut the door so no light would spill into the room. I settled myself in my niche. I filmed ten minutes of antics with the motorbike and managed to get close-ups of each of the lads. The main aim of the game seemed to be revving it up as hard as possible then racing up the Close and squealing to a halt with a skid. There weren't any girls hanging about. I wondered what they were doing while their boyfriends and brothers played Easy Rider.

There was no sign of life at all from the Ibrahims. I couldn't tell if the lights were on in the house, all the curtains were drawn and no-one came or went. Things were quiet for a while apart from the sound of a child wailing and two dogs barking a duet. A plane took off overhead, we weren't far from the airport. When it had climbed out of sight and the sound had faded I could only hear the child crying.

Later there was a burst of thumping music from a car passing on the main road. A man walked past with a small, Scottish terrier on a lead. The dog stopped and squatted, left a turd on the pavement. The man waited, no sign of concern about him. I should have filmed him, I thought to myself, sent it in somewhere and got him fined. Dog fouling seemed to have reached epidemic proportions in Manchester, every trip to the park followed by cleaning up the kids shoes with an old toothbrush and disinfectant. Horrible.

A woman pushing a buggy came from the bottom of the Close. Out late or walking round trying to get the baby to sleep?

I was getting stiff and the wig was driving me mad. I took it off and scratched my head furiously, plonked it back on. I was starting to feel drowsy too. Reckoned I needed a caffeine boost. I'd brought a snack with me too, cheese butty and a slab of flapjack. I'd have those, stoke myself up.

The door to Mr Poole's back room was ajar. I knocked and went in.

'Wow!' It was like a library or a social history museum, books lined three walls, the fourth displayed posters and banners from past campaigns. Ban the Bomb, Support Nalgo, Victory to the Miners. A large table in the centre of the room was stacked with magazines, papers and more books. Mr Poole sat at the table in a high-backed chair.

'My study.'

'You've quite a collection.'

'Yes, it'll go to the Mechanics Institute when I'm gone. Lot of these are originals, out of print now. And the pamphlets and leaflets, can't get them anywhere else. I'm still cataloguing the more recent material.'

'How've you got hold of it all?'

'Well, I've kept the items that have come my way, through the union, been a shop steward all my life when I was in work. And things from the Tenants and then the different campaigns and such like. The rest people have passed on to me, knowing I'd a collection.' I thought of Lisa MacNeice with her hens.

'One chap I knew, Archie Ferguson, he was a big man in the unions at Ferranti. Well, Archie died last year and his wife Betty rang me.'

'"George," she says, "I've half-a-dozen boxes here, Archie's papers and he wanted you to have them.' I got round there and she's got a room full. He kept everything – minutes going back forty years, notices of meetings, old rule books, correspondence. I could have filled a ship with it. Well, I found what was worth keeping, and that took some doing, mind you, and I told her to get the scouts to take the rest for their paper collections.'

I smiled. 'I'd like to get a cup of coffee.'

'I'll do it,' he pulled himself up.

'I don't mind,' I volunteered, 'if you show me where you keep everything.'

'I'll show you now and then if you need anything later you know what's what.'

Back in my viewing position I sipped coffee and demolished my snack. I felt an initial wave of fatigue as all the blood rushed to my stomach. I stretched and yawned and fooled around with the camera a bit. It was dark now, the scene illuminated in moody orange from the streetlights.

Two cars drove down the Close at high speed. People spilled out at the bottom. There was a lot of shouting and snatches of a song. 'Engerland, Eng-er-land.' I felt my spine tense. I wondered whether Mrs Ahmed was listening too, waiting for the trouble to begin.

The group walked up the street and gathered on the pavement outside the Ibrahims'. I began to film. There were six in all. The twins and Micky Whittaker were there and another teenager, seriously overweight and with a shaved head. I filmed the group and the scene before cutting in for close-ups. It was obvious who the men were, they closely resembled their offspring: Mr Brennan, balding with thin patches of flame coloured hair, short, stocky, grinning a lot; his accomplice Whittaker, tall and stooping with lank, shoulder length hair and a thin moustache. He wore a denim jacket and torn jeans and looked as if he was freezing. He shivered frequently, stood with his shoulders hunched, arms crossed, hands tucked under his armpits.

A joint was passing round and the Whittaker boy passed round cans of super-strong lager. One of the twins sprayed the other with foam and got cuffed across the face by his father who screeched at him. 'Don't waste it, yer fuckin' pillock.'

The teenagers glugged at the cans, toked on the joint. They moved closer to the house. Then in turn they ran up and hammered on the door, screaming and shouting. After a minute or two they'd swap places, like a sick relay race. The men began to sing a dirge; 'Go home, go home, fuck off, go home...' to the tune of Amazing Grace. As the ditty finished they broke into a fast chant, obscene and racist. I caught fragments, I didn't know how much the microphone on the camera would pick up, enough I hoped. 'Coons and wogs, they eat dogs, ay allez oop…'

I hated them. I wanted to silence them, kick their stupid, racist heads in. Not a civilised response, I know, just a gut reaction.

Next time, if there had to be a next time, I'd leave the window ajar to catch more of what they were saying.

I heard a movement behind me – Mr Poole opening the door. He'd had the sense to turn the landing light out.

'I've spotted Brennan and the twins and Whittaker and his boy. There's another lad as well, shaved head, overweight?'

'Bunter, that's what they call him. Darren is his real name. He lives next door but one. He's a bit slow. They lead him on, that lot, take advantage of him and he gets into trouble. He doesn't understand half of what's going on – just wants to be part of the gang. Grown men.' I heard him sigh. 'What, on God's earth, makes them do this?' Frustration strained his voice.

The songs and the chants went on, more cans were consumed. The empty ones were hurled at the house, the group cheered whenever a window was hit. They repeatedly went up and kicked the front door.

'I'm going to ring the police now,' I said to

Mr Poole, 'I don't want it to get any worse.'

It took the police twenty minutes to arrive. In the meantime I filmed Darren peeing against the Ibrahim's door, egged on by the others who cheered when he'd finished. I was shaking, my teeth gritted shut. Where was Mrs Ahmed and her three children? Settled in the kitchen as far as possible from the threats at the front? Could she get the children off to sleep and sit and listen alone? Or did she put the telly on to drown them out; try and follow the stories from the images, the babble of English hard for her to understand? Did the shouts and thumps bring back the horrors she had lived through in Somalia, swamping her with fear making her hands shake and her mouth dry? How did she cope?

'Get a chair next time,' yelled Brennan, 'do it through the letterbox.'

'She might suck it for yer,' roared Whittaker.

The group howled with laughter. The twins made wanking motions with their fists. Where were the bloody police?

At last the squad car appeared and as it drove down the Close the gang became quiet. They moved nearer together, ribaldry over.

The police got out of the car. I kept filming. Brennan greeted one of them by name. 'Alright, Benny.' He said there'd been reports of a disturbance. Innocent faces were pulled.

'Carl Benson,' Mr Poole whispered, referring to the younger policeman, 'local lad.'

'I live on here,' said Brennan, 'this is my street. Can't a man walk down his own street?'

'Free country, innit?' asked Whittaker. 'Used to be anyway, till we were swamped by immigrants, taking houses and jobs.'

'Come on, now, time for home,' said the other policeman.

'Why, eh? Why?' Brennan was all outrage, hands spread wide. 'We haven't done nothing, this is harassment, this is.'

There was no reply. The police stood there. Implacable but not looking half as hard as the men they faced.

It was Whittaker who gave the signal at last. 'Freezin' out here anyway. Funny smell an' all. Like a farmyard.' One of the twins snorted. I saw Carl Benson's face tighten, his adam's apple bob.

'Got a dirty movie back at the house, few more cans.' They began to walk away.

'Darren?' A woman's voice calling.

'Darren, come on now.' Darren's face fell, he turned away from the group, rolled his shoulders in an embarrassed shrug.

'Go on, Bunter,' teased Micky Whittaker, 'beddy-byes.'

The police stood and watched until the group had gone into the houses at the bottom of the Close. The older man got in the car. Carl Benson crossed to Mr Poole's. We went downstairs and Mr Poole let him in. I confirmed that I'd called the police and told him what I'd seen, he noted it all down in his book. I explained that I was video-recording events for a possible court case – it was all on tape. Yes, I would be happy to be a witness if required.

'It's Carl, isn't it?' Mr Poole said.

'Yeah,' he blushed a little.

'How's your Mum doing?'

'Alright, they've put a ramp in now and a downstairs bathroom. It's a lot better.'

''Bout time and all. Give her my regards.'

'Yeh, right. Best be off.'

'Glad it was them,' said Mr Poole as we returned to the kitchen. 'There's one copper round here and all he ever wanted to do was race round in fast cars – now he does it for a living – like the Sweeney. If he wasn't a copper he'd be a villain.'

'It's possible to be both at the same time.'

'Aye and he probably is. But Carl's a good lad.'

I left Mr Poole to his filing and went back upstairs.

I was tired now, just a couple of hours to go until Mr Ibrahim was due back. Precious little happening. A couple more dog walkers. I yawned a lot and did some more stretching.

At twenty past two a private hire cab arrived and stopped outside the house opposite. A man got out; dark coat and hat, moustache. Mr Ibrahim, I presumed. He knocked on the door. I realised they probably used bolts as well as locks so she'd have to let him in. The door opened and he slipped through. I caught no glimpse of her. The taxi drove away.

Time for home.

I packed up the camcorder and cleared the bits into my bag. Downstairs I looked in on Mr Poole. He was still at his table but sitting back in the large, upholstered chair. Eyes closed, mouth open, snoring softly. With each snore the loose skin around his chin shivered. I went across and touched his shoulder.

'Mr Poole? I'm going now.'

He blinked a few times and shut his mouth; rubbed his face with his hand.

'I'll see myself out. Don't forget to ring me whenever there's any bother. Goodnight.'

The roads were quiet driving home. Once I'd gone a little way I took the wig and glasses off. I wondered whether the footage I'd got would be enough for Mandy Bellows to take the troublemakers to court. Surely it would.

Verbal abuse – overly racist, threatening behaviour, attacking property. I noted that the men had watched and spurred on the youths but neither Brennan nor Whittaker had actually gone up to the Ibrahims' house. Intentionally – so they couldn't be accused? But my recollection was that injunctions could apply to tenants and to their families, so even though the teenagers were minors they could still be the subject of a court order. And if they carried on with the anti-social behaviour the property could be re-possessed.

I reckoned there was plenty to go on but it would be up to the solicitors at the Town Hall.

Home was still, quiet. Laura was there, I could always tell from the smell of her perfume. Overpowering, she must chuck bucketfuls of it on. Acted on me like nerve gas. Must have stripped the linings of her nostrils so she couldn't even smell how strong it was. Left the rest of us reeling. I was being uncharitable, I was tired.

Bed felt blissful. I closed my eyes. Images from the evening flickered through my mind; the faces of the group, drunk and giddy with cruelty, Whittaker shivering in his denims, Darren beaming as they all applauded. Mr Poole's voice, raw with emotion. 'What, on God's earth, makes them do this?'

Chapter Eight

The weekend was a blur of domesticity. Saturday afternoon I took the kids to Castlefield. The Museum of Science and Industry were hosting a dinosaur exhibition. Tom was beside himself with excitement. Maddie kept trying to act cool about it, 'dinosaurs are for babies, Mum,' but when we entered the Jurassic environment her face said it all. The place was done out like a swamp complete with soundtrack of blood-curdling roars. The animatronic dinosaurs had both Tom and Maddie enthralled. And when one particularly nasty one actually spit at Tom I thought he'd wet himself with glee. After a trip to the shop we visited our old favourites; the steam hall with its missive engines complete with life-size T. Rex this time and the interactive section upstairs where the kids played with magnets and mirrors and shadows and sounds. By then I was too tired to take them to the Air and Space building, Appollo and the Daleks would have to wait for another day.

I had done a little bit of work that morning. I watched the video – it was blurry at times and the light wasn't brilliant but it was adequate in terms of seeing what was actually going on. The sound was muffled, I might need to tell people what the youths had been shouting, but even without the words the pictures said it all. Reviewing the behaviour of the gang made me tense with anger again. The cruelty of their taunts and the ugliness of their behaviour revolted me. I tried to work out how they must feel about themselves to be so ready to attack others?

I dispatched a courier with the videotape for Mandy Bellows. I included a note asking her to let me know as soon as possible whether the tape was all they needed. I could then return the camcorder.

I also checked the e-mail for answers from potential Jennifer Pickerings; everyone I'd contacted had replied and none of them was the right person. The woman in Scarborough even referred to the fact that she'd been contacted before, by a member of the family. Roger, I presumed. Of course he'd have checked for her online – it was his field of work but I consoled myself that at least I was being thorough.

On the Saturday night it was dry enough to have a bonfire and burn the debris from the garden along with some scraps of wood from the cellar that Ray had no use for. There was also an old wooden cupboard, riddled with woodworm, that had been rotting in the shed. The kids took great delight in helping to break it up.

There's an old paved area at the bottom of the garden in one corner. I'm not sure why it was laid there as it's no suntrap but it works fine for the children to ride bikes on and it's ideal for bonfires. I used a couple of rows of broken flagstones to form a small circular fireplace and then I built a pyramid of scrunched up paper, kindling and sticks. I lit the fire. It was smoky at first until it burnt off the moisture then the twigs crackled and hissed and I gradually added larger pieces of wood.

I called Ray and Laura and they brought out the food; baked potatoes with cheese and tomato sauce and sticks of carrot and celery to crunch on. Maddie and Tom drank dandelion and burdock, the rest of us had some bottled beer that Laura had contributed.

'When's bonfire night?' asked Maddie.

'A while yet,' I said.

'How many weeks?'

'Can we have fireworks,' said Tom, 'very, very loud ones?'

'I hate loud ones. We should just have sparklers. Is it next week?'

'No, about six weeks.'

'That's ages,' she complained.

'Look in the fire,' I said, 'what shapes can you see?'

The chunks of wood were burning slowly, revealing their intricate grid design, charring into little squares, echoing the structure of bark. The patterns always reminded me of the fine network of lines on our skin, too.

'A witch's face,' said Maddie, 'and a little

house. There,' she pointed.

'I can see a dog being sick,' Tom boasted.

'You're sick,' said Maddie.

'And a willy,' he found this absolutely hilarious and nearly choked on his dandelion and burdock.

We let the children carefully add wood to the fire, warning them not to throw anything on which could knock it all down and put out the flames.

Laura and Ray sat close and every so often Tom would launch himself onto Ray's knee and wriggle off after he'd got a bit of attention.

'We used to have huge bonfires at home,' said Laura to Tom, 'so big the men had to climb up ladders to put the guy on top.'

'Where was it?' I asked. I knew she'd been raised in the country and she still had a soft burr to her voice not common in Manchester.

'Lincolnshire,' she said, 'middle of nowhere.'

'They're all inbred like mad,' Ray joshed.

She punched him on the arm.

'Did you live on a farm?'

'No, my Dad worked on a farm nearby but we didn't live there, we had a house in the village.'

'Did you have to go to school?' asked Maddie.

'Yes, and do you know how many children were in my school?'

'How many?' Maddie's eyes danced.

'How many?' echoed Tom.

'Twelve.'

'Twelve!' I couldn't imagine it.

Laura shivered.

'You cold?' Ray asked her.

'A bit.'

Not surprising. We were all togged up in woolly jumpers or fleeces and Laura had a short sleeved top on.

'I'll get you a coat.'

'I'll be alright.'

'Don't be daft,' he stood up, 'you'll freeze.' He came back with a woollen jacket which she wrapped round herself. It dwarfed her. She was only small, slim too. Fine featured with long blonde hair, grey eyes, a brown birthmark the size of a cherry on one cheek. Ray had met her at college, she was an assistant to their administrator.

'Tom,' Ray warned his son who stood poised to chuck a large block of wood into the fire. 'That's too big, find a stick.' I could see the flames reflected in Tom's dark eyes, slivers of light shining on his glossy curls.

He grinned and dropped the wood.

Maddie sidled onto my knee and we sat quietly for a while. Maybe it would be possible for Laura to move in with us, it would be better than Ray and Tom moving out. I'd have to get used to sharing my home with a couple, get used to their intimacy. But would she want to live like this? With Maddie and me as well as Ray and Tom, and Sheila, our lodger, to boot? Was there space? I was assuming that she'd move into Ray's bedroom but in her shoes I'd want a room of my own; she had a flat to herself after all. Giving that up. We couldn't ask Sheila to leave, we had an agreement. We'd have to move the kids' playroom, maybe put it in the cellar – or bring their beds down, put them in the playroom. But then they'd be sleeping on a different floor, I didn't like that idea…

'Mummy,' Maddie shouted, 'can I have a drink or what!' She'd been repeating it and I was miles away – worrying.

I tried to explain myself to Diane when we met up for a drink the following evening. 'I'm uncomfortable with them. Even with Ray, he's changed. I'm not jealous, you know I've never really fancied Ray. It's more of a feeling of being pushed out. Perhaps it's envy? And then I keep thinking how awful it'll be if they move out.'

'Why?'

'It's worked so well, especially looking after the children. Tom and Maddie are close, we're all close. I'd miss Tom dreadfully. We're like a family, it's like a divorce waiting to happen.'

'Have you asked Ray?'

'Asked him what?'

'If they're making plans?'

'You sound just like his mother,' I scoffed.

'Well, have you?' she persisted.

'Diane, I can hardly talk to him about anything at the moment, he's gone all vague and absent-minded.'

'It must be lurve,' she joked and rolled her eyes.

'It's irritating whatever it is.'

'You should ask him. Tell him what your worries are. All you need to say is that you'd like him to let you know if he's considering any big changes. After all it does affect you and Maddie, like you say.' She rattled the ice cubes in her glass.

'Yes.' Reluctant. Why? Because I didn't want Ray to see how vulnerable I could be? Because I didn't want to make a fool of myself? Because he might confirm my fears?

'Is Laura around a lot?'

'Yeah, more than before or he goes to her flat. She's nice – well, she's alright, I've nothing against the woman.'

Diane chortled.

'What?'

'You should hear yourself. Talk about back-handed compliments.'

'Well, it's not her, she's not the problem. It's the situation. Whoever Ray was seeing it would feel the same, if it was this intense. I can get on with her OK...'

Diane gave me a look.

'I can! OK we're not big buddies but I never see her without Ray so there's no chance to get to know her properly.' I drained my glass. I wanted another.

'Do that then, arrange to see just her.'

'Oh, I couldn't do that. She'd think I was weird. And Ray would hate it.'

'Why's it so weird?'

'Well, it's their relationship, Laura's there to be with Ray not get to know the house-mates.'

'But if she's thinking of moving in...'

'OK. Yes, if she was moving in I'd want to get to know her, not just as Ray's girlfriend – but she may not be.' I finished lamely.

'So, talk to him. I've been here before. Deja vu.'

'Get us a drink.'

She was looking all exasperated.

I raised my eyebrows. 'Please.'

When she returned I switched topics. Told her about my latest cases. I know she won't blab about it to anyone. She was suitably appalled at the account I gave her of the attacks on the Ibrahim family.

'How quickly can the council act, then?'

'I don't know. It'll be up to their solicitors to decide if the evidence is strong enough. Then they'll either get injunctions outlining how the behaviour of the parties has to change – not approaching the Ibrahims' house or family, that sort of thing – or they'll go for terminating the tenancy and they'll repossess the properties.'

'That would be best, wouldn't it? Doesn't sound as though they'd pay any attention to an injunction.'

'Yes. They might even move the Ibrahims in the meantime. It's horrendous what they're having to put up with.' I had a drink, enjoying the taste of the beer. 'The other thing I'm on is a missing person. Well, sort of. She left for university in 1976 and hasn't been seen since.'

'What, not by anybody?'

'No. But nobody's been looking, either. She was pregnant so it's possible that she just went off and had her baby and created a new life for herself or had it adopted or had an abortion. Take your pick.'

'How do you find someone after all that time?'

'Slowly,' I smiled. 'It's not easy but I'm hoping the university will have a reference for where she went and failing that I'll try the General Records Office for births and marriages.'

'So who's your client?'

'Her brother, he's a lot younger, there were just the two of them. Father's dead now and their mother's dying of cancer. I think he wants to give them a chance to make amends. I suppose also if he doesn't find her he's really on his own, no family anymore. But the mother has no interest in finding her daughter. Snapped his head off when he suggested it.'

'Ah.'

'So, if I do find her I think there's going to have to be a lot of delicate negotiations before there's any death-bed reunion or anything like that. Do you remember that really hot summer? Seventy-six. The drought. That's when she left home.'

'Yes, I was in Yorkshire, we had stand-pipes in the street. Doesn't half make you careful with it – luggin' it about.'

'My Dad drained the bathwater down a pipe hung out the window to use on his vegetables. Everyone else had given up. The ground was rock hard. Long time ago.' I took a drink. 'So, I'm busy, busy enough. And you?'

'More of the same.' Diane was working on a collection of textile pieces for a Bank and continuing to create her own prints as well. Her hands were stained a light blue and there were traces of crimson under a couple of her nails. Inky hands were always a good sign with Diane. Proof of production. She was most ratty when she hadn't had chance to muck about with paint as she put it.

'And how is the darling Desmond?' Her new man. Success in the lonely hearts columns.

'Fine,' she said. 'He's really nice. Very sweet.'

'I hear a *but*, in there somewhere.'

She looked despondent, tugged at her hair, a rather nasty silver blonde this month with a single extension that came dangerously close to dipping in her drink.

'But…' I prompted.

'It's not him. It's…'

'What?' Silence. Oh, hell, must be something awful. 'You're not pregnant?' Diane's worst nightmare.

'No, it's not that. You know how careful I am. Promise you won't preach…'

'Preach?' What on earth was she on about it. She wasn't usually this coy. 'Just tell me.'

'I had a phone call. From Ben.'

'Oh, no,' I groaned.

'Sal,' she said crossly.

'Well, it's just that he made you so unhappy.' I fiddled with my beer glass.

'Not on purpose,' she retorted.

'Why did he ring?'

'Talk,' she said in a small voice. 'He's engaged.'

'Oh, great. So he wanted to tell you all about it, did he?'

'Sal, don't.'

'Sorry.' I bit my tongue.

'He's met someone through work, she's based in Brussels. He said … he's been thinking about me a lot.'

I resisted the temptation to raise my eyes to heaven and groan.

'He wanted to meet up, see me again.'

119

What was wrong with the guy? Cold feet?

'What did you say?'

She sighed. 'I said I could do tomorrow.'

'You're going to see him?' I was aghast. Ben and Diane had been happy briefly before their relationship got bogged down by different expectations. Ben wanted commitment, more specifically he wanted children. Diane didn't, never had and wasn't going to change her mind. For Ben that sounded the death knell to the liaison. After the break-up Diane was very upset, she missed him terribly, she pined. Time had helped, other men had come and gone. She mentioned him less and less. I assumed she was over him. Wrong.

'Why?' I asked her.

'Because, I still feel...' she hesitated, '...I still love him,' she said simply, 'just hearing his voice was ... I know it's pathetic but no one else has ever made me feel like he does.'

'He made you feel bloody awful for months on end.'

'I know,' she glared at me.

'Why does he want to see you? Did he say?'

'Not really. He's on the brink of a big step, I think he wants to make sure he's made the right decision.'

It sounded awful to me, checking over an ex-girlfriend just to make sure that your fiancee is a better bet. But I kept mum. There was an awkward pause in the conversation. I searched for something constructive to say.

'Is he coming up to Manchester?'

'No,' she said, 'I told him I'd rather meet on neutral ground. He's booked a hotel in London. I might get a chance to see some of the galleries. Haven't been to the Tate for years.'

'Does his fiancee know?'

'Single rooms, Sal. What do you think I am?'

A chump, seeing as you're asking. And you didn't answer my question. After a night on the town, a nice meal, fine wine, some heartfelt talk, I couldn't see separate rooms being an obstacle. Diane had just told me how much she still cared for the man. Of course she'd want to sleep with him.

'I knew you'd do this,' she said.

'What?'

'Go all moral on me.'

'I just don't want you to get hurt again, that's all.'

'I'm a big girl,' she said.

I began to smile. 'So I can see.' I nodded

at Diane's statuesque figure.

She laughed. A truce. I didn't dare ask whether Desmond knew about Ben or the coming reunion. I knew I'd hear all about it in good time.

Chapter Nine

Monday morning had that crisp autumn feel to it. Not cold enough for gloves yet but no longer balmy. Monday was Ray's regular slot for doing the school run so I was able to set off for Sheffield as soon as I was ready. The journey took longer than I expected. Much of it was over the peaks via the Snake Pass, which gives some indication of its nature. On many of the winding sections overtaking was prohibited and I got stuck behind a slow climbing lorry. The scenery was exhilarating especially on the tops above the tree line where I could see moorland and grass rippling over the hills and dropping down in folds over the valleys and gulleys.

I usually pride myself on being punctual, part of the professionalism I want to bring to the job but I knew I'd be late. Not that Caroline Cunningham was going anywhere with an infection like that.

Towards the end of the journey I joined the motorway and was soon negotiating my way along the dual carriageways and ring-roads of the city. There was still plenty of evidence of Sheffield's history as the steel-making capital of the nation. Tracts of derelict factories and warehouses, evidence of re-building and demolition and the great water towers which I assumed were prev-iously used by the smelting works.

I got lost twice but finally made it to my destination. Caroline Cunningham lived in a row of terraced houses banked up on a long, incredibly steep hill. We're not used to hills in Manchester nor the vistas they pro-vide. I could see the panorama of the city and beyond the jumble of buildings, chim-neys and roads to the surrounding hills.

Caroline Cunningham bore little resem-blance to the pictures I'd seen at Lisa's, even accounting for her bleary eyes and washed out complexion. The long red hair was long gone replaced by a short bobbed hairstyle in rich brown. She wore gold rimmed glasses, dangly black earrings, a fleecy grey top and black leggings.

A cat wound its way around my legs as I tried to get along the narrow hallway.

'Jasper!' she scooped the cat up. 'He's been trodden on so much he ought to look like a doormat by now. Come in here.'

The rooms were small, two up-two down as far as I could tell with a minute kitchen. The decor suited the original features; a richly tiled fireplace with cast iron surround and a brass coal scuttle matched dark patterned wallpaper and the jade green of the picture rail. The net curtains were heavy cream lace patterned with birds of paradise and there were pictures of Old Sheffield on the walls and an embroidered sampler. 'Be good sweet maid and let who will be clever.' Girls' education circa 1900.

I accepted the offer of a cup of tea and fussed with the cats while Caroline brewed up.

'So you've seen Lisa, she still in Chester?'

'Yes.'

'She's working, yet?'

I didn't grasp the 'yet'. 'I don't know, we just talked about Jennifer.'

Caroline handed me tea, a sceptical look on her face. I wasn't sure why.

'Lisa hadn't heard from her, nothing since seventy-six.'

'Neither have I.'

'It seems that she left her course at Keele that first term.'

Caroline settled herself on the chintz sofa. 'Yeah.'

'Have you any idea where she might have gone?'

'No,' she coughed violently and blew her nose on a tissue.

It was a dead end. I had a wave of despondency. Why had I bothered coming all this way? Just to have confirmed what I already knew? I could have done it over the phone. But a phone call is rarely as good as face to face contact for getting people to open up, or for spotting discrepancies between what they say and what their body language reveals. I was there at Caroline's to do my job as well as I could. Just get on with it.

'Did you know she was pregnant?'

'Lisa told me,' she sounded a bit miffed about that. 'I was away most of the summer. My parents had a place in Brittany. I missed all the action. When I came back Lisa told me about Jenny and I felt really sorry for her, she should have been on the pill. I've often wondered what she did about it. If I'd been in her shoes I'd have had an abortion, especially you know, with the father...'

'What?'

She flushed slightly, blew her nose again. 'He was black, wasn't he. It wasn't like it is now. And her father would have gone mad if he knew. We never could work out if she'd told them. Lisa said she hadn't. But when Jennifer never went back I thought she probably had told them and they'd just cut her off. He had a breakdown as well didn't he, Mr Pickering, had to give up work, that could have been why.' There was a triumphant smile on her lips. 'Especially if Jenny insisted on keeping the child.'

'You say her father would have been very upset, was he closer to her than her mother?' I tried to picture Jennifer as a Daddy's Girl and failed.

'No,' she shuffled on the sofa, 'but he had very strong opinions. He wouldn't approve of people inter-marrying. Stick to your own. Of course he was the leader at that Church as well so it'd have been awful for him that way too.'

And for Jennifer? Caroline seemed to have little compassion.

'He had a point really,' she sipped her drink. 'It wasn't so bad back then but it's all gone too far really. I mean, I go to the shops

126

round here and I'm the only person speaking English. Little Pakistan. And no-one dares to say anything about it. Everything's so softly softly. What about the right to free speech?'

'So her father was a racist?' I asked her coldly. 'What about her mother?'

She shrugged. 'Went along with his principles I suppose. She was very old-fashioned.'

'How did Jennifer get along with her parents?'

'Not well,' she wheezed a little and cleared her throat. 'They were very strict. She couldn't wait to leave home.'

'Were you and Jennifer close?'

'Seemed like it then, the four of us went around together, Lisa, Jenny, Frances and me. But once we'd all left school, we made new friends. I came here, Lisa had a place at Crewe. I went to Frances's wedding,' she added, 'and Lisa's – that was a right farce.'

'Why?'

'Lisa getting married.' She jerked her head as if I needed reminding about something. 'Thank God they never had kids.'

My incomprehension must have shown.

'You know,' she prompted.

I didn't.

'She's gay, isn't she, a lesbian. There was all that stuff in the papers, last year, that was her.'

I shook my head. I didn't know what had been in the papers.

Caroline's eyes brightened with the gossip. 'She was a teacher, further education college. Word got out she was a lesbian, right, she was seeing one of her students,' she grimaced, 'it was all over the papers, *The Sun* and everything. She had to leave her job. There was a lot of Muslim students – they won't stand for it. Don't you remember?'

What, one rabid tabloid witch-hunt from among all the others? No. It did help explain Lisa's caution when I'd got in touch and her hesitation when I'd asked her how close she had been to Jennifer.

'I'd no idea she was like that,' Caroline continued, 'if I'd known when we were at school.' She twisted her mouth with distaste. 'We slept at each others' houses and everything. I hadn't a clue. It's the husband I feel sorry for, getting married and then … what he must have been through.'

I stared at her. How the hell did she know I wasn't 'like that' too? I was more than eager to conclude my interview with Caroline

Cunningham. She had rapidly become my least favourite of Jennifer's friends. But I still had a few more questions to ask her.

'When did you last see Jennifer?'

'Before I went on holiday to Brittany.'

'So you didn't see her before she left for Keele?'

'No. Should have done though. It was my birthday on the 14th. We were all going to go for a meal and then onto the Ritz in town. We'd been planning it for ages. Sort of last fling before we all went off to uni. She never came. I was a bit pissed off to be honest. But then when I heard about the baby I thought maybe she couldn't face it. She could have sent a card or something though. It's like she just gave up on everybody. Who needs friends like that?'

'Perhaps she'd gone for an abortion, thought people would disapprove.'

'Not us. Well, apart from Frances who was holier than thou about things like that. There were two girls in school had abortions in the sixth form, everyone knew. It was OK. People felt sorry for them.'

'So why do you think Jennifer dropped all her friends? Never got in touch.'

She shrugged. 'Because we reminded her of home, of her parents? She wanted a new start? Who knows? We thought it was quite exciting at the time, once it turned out that she'd left the university and she wouldn't tell anyone where she was living. Romantic. Jenny cutting herself off from her family. I think we imagined her swanning back when she'd made a success of her life, rubbing their noses in it, but she never did, did she? Sank without trace.'

'Did Jennifer ever talk about wanting to live in a particular place, somewhere she'd go if she got the chance?'

'No, not that I remember,' she fished for a tissue and wiped her nose.

'Were there any friends or family you heard of in other places?'

'No. I don't think they had any other family. No aunties and uncles and that. Her mother had been an only child and she'd grown up on a farm miles from anywhere. Jennifer reckoned that's partly why she was so strict because of her own upbringing.'

'But they let her go off to Knebworth, didn't they?' I recalled the snapshots of Jennifer and Lisa by their tent.

'She never told them it was Knebworth. They thought the pair of them were camping in the Peak district. Girl Guide stuff.'

I nodded. I checked back over my notes to

see if I'd missed anything. 'Well, I think that's about it. Thanks for seeing me.' I got to my feet.

'Have you seen Frances?'

'Tomorrow.'

'She never left Manchester, did her course there, got a job, then the wedding and started a family. Seems happy enough. And it's Roger Pickering who wants you to find Jennifer?'

'Yes.'

'John and Roger were at school together,' she said, 'he was always painfully shy. They say he's doing quite well for himself now, in computers. Surprising really,' she blew her nose.

I waited to see if there was going to be any further significance to her mean little observations but she didn't add anything. I didn't feel any compunction to give any more away to Caroline. More grist for her gossip mill. Besides which Roger was my client and I had a duty to respect confidentiality in my work.

I said a brisk goodbye and she saw me out.

I stood by my car for a minute, let my eyes wander over the view, breathed in the cold air to take away the dirty feeling I'd picked up during the encounter.

Once I was back on the road heading for Snake Pass I felt as though I'd escaped from something. It was hard to imagine how Caroline and Lisa could have got along so well at school. Maybe Caroline's insidious opinions hadn't been formed back than, maybe she'd been corrupted at university, falling in with the wrong crowd, flirting with the fascists, learning to see everyone else as different, inferior, threatening. I wondered how she would judge the antics of the Brennans and the Whittakers. I thought she'd probably be appalled – not recognising that her own attitudes helped create a climate in which their violent racism could flourish.

I was up on the hilltops when my mobile rang. I pulled into a passing place and stopped the car to take the call.

'It's Lisa MacNeice here, you said to ring if I thought of anything,' her voice was tinny on the phone.

'Yes?'

'Well, I remembered something, I've been thinking about it all since you came ... I can't see how it'll help, though.'

'Go on.'

'It was on the phone, not long before

Jenny went. She was upset, I thought it was about the pregnancy and everything but she kept calling her father a hypocrite, she wouldn't say why. She was really angry.'

It was hardly a big break.

'Was it unusual, her calling him names, getting upset?'

'Well, she called him all sorts, you know what teenagers are like. He was big on morals and what he called decent behaviour and all that and she hated his conservatism, his prejudice. But this felt different. She rang me up to tell me, for a start and at first I thought she'd told him about the baby and he'd been horrible about it and she was calling him a hypocrite because he wasn't being a Christian and forgiving her. Mind you his particular Church never seemed very tolerant.'

'Maybe he told her to get an abortion?' I suggested.

'Yes, that would fit. But the thing is, I asked Jenny if she'd told them and she said no, not yet. She said it was something else.'

'You got the impression something had happened, her father had said something or done something that she thought was hypocritical?'

'Yes.'

'But not connected to her pregnancy?'

'No.'

'And this was just before she left?'

'Yes, it's so hard to be sure after all these years but it was one of the last times we spoke, if not the last. At the time you're just talking you don't expect to be quizzed on it decades after, you don't know it might be important.'

'I know,' I reassured her, 'you've done well to remember it at all. And if anything else comes up do call me.'

There was no milk at the office so I called home for some and collected a cheese and vegetable pastie that had come of age. If I didn't eat it for lunch I'd have to bin it. There was a bank statement and a wodge of junk mail for me in the Dobson's hall-way. Somehow my name had reached a list in catalogue land and I was being bombarded with free gift offers, new customer bribes and the promise of 250,000 pounds in cash or 5,000 per year for life if I'd only take a catalogue and buy something. I dumped everything but the bank statement. I made a coffee before I opened it. I looked at it, closed my eyes and took a rallying breath then filed it. It wouldn't seem so bad in a couple of days.

I updated my notes and rang Roger Pickering. It was about time I told him what I'd found out about his sister. We arranged to meet the following day after I'd seen Frances Delaney. I wondered whether that would be a waste of time but unlike Caroline Cunningham she lived locally so it needn't take me long to see her and then I'd have finished with Jennifer's friends. I worked on a draft report for Roger so he could see what I'd been doing with his money. Would he want to retain me when I was getting nowhere fast? I'd have to be honest with him about my fading hopes. Even if Keele did give me Jennifer's forwarding address there would be twenty odd years of moving house to trace and pursue. It would be time-consuming and there'd be no guarantee of success.

The phone rang. 'Sal, it's Mandy. Thank you for the tape.'

'Can you use it?'

'They're dithering. I'm not going to have an answer till later this week. I get the impression there's some uncertainty between the two solicitors who've seen it and they want to discuss it with the boss.'

'But it's clear enough isn't it? You can

make out who's involved and...'

'Yes. That's not the issue. They won't go to court unless they're ninety-nine percent certain of winning. It's out of my hands now until I get word from them, so hang onto the camera in the meantime.'

'What is it that they're not sure about?' I demanded. 'It's obviously harassment, you can hear most of what they're shouting, all the racist abuse. And they attack the property, too – all the kicking the door...'

'Yes, it's awful,' she agreed, 'but sometimes they need to prove the violence is sustained, that it's an ongoing problem.'

'There's all the police call-outs.'

'Sal, it's not up to me. I wish it were.'

'I'm sorry, I know.'

'I'll get back to you, as soon as I hear one way or the other. I hope it'll be later in the week but I can't promise.'

I paced about a bit after that, seriously pissed off. I couldn't settle to my report for Roger Pickering or any other paperwork. It was just after two. I locked up and went home. The house was a mess after the weekend. I tidied and hoovered the lounge and swept the stairs and the kitchen floor. I'd worked up a sweat by the time I'd done and created a bit of order to make up for the fact that out there everything was crazy and out of control.

At nine thirty that evening Mr Poole rang me. 'Can you come,' he said urgently, 'there's trouble brewing.'

Chapter Ten

My stomach tightened. I told him I'd be there as soon as possible. I slapped on the wig and glasses and the long mac, got the sports bag from my room and told Ray where I was going. He looked at me for a while and for an awful moment I thought he was going to ask me if I'd changed anything but he finally figured it out.

'Is it fancy dress?'

'Undercover, reduces the risk of any dodgy types coming after me,' I tried to make it sound jokey.

'Good,' he said. His face closed down. There wasn't any warmth in the comment. I knew he was thinking about previous occasions when my work had come far too close to home. It was an area we skirted round now. I had a rush of irritation with him. The past was over and done with. How long was he going to cradle his disapproval? We needed to talk about it, but not then. I was in a hurry.

Traffic was light and I reached Canterbury Close in fifteen minutes. It was drizzling, the soft, steady veil of damp that Manchester does so well, creating balls of diffuse orange light around the street lamps.

I could see a huddle of people outside the Ibrahims'. There was a van parked outside Mr Poole's house so I drove on and found a space further down the Close. The fine rain made it hard to see clearly what was going on. I fiddled with my rear-view mirror and pretended to mess with my hair. Though there's not a lot to do with a plain grey wig. I could see the Brennan twins and Micky Whittaker, no sign of the two adults or Darren. A fourth boy was bouncing a football from one knee to the other.

I got out of the car and locked up. I felt the attention swivel my way and a silence stretched the seconds. My shoulders tensed up and my stomach contracted. The football slammed against the far side of my car.

'Hey,' I shouted, 'pack it in.'

Someone echoed me in a falsetto voice.

There were jeers from the group. It would be unwise to antagonise them further. I needed to get inside, set the camera up, do my job. I walked quickly towards Mr Poole's. One of the twins intercepted me at the gate.

'Where you think you're going?' He dripped insolence.

I moved to side-step him and he shadowed me. I was close enough to see the fuzzy hair on his upper lip, the cold sore at one corner of this mouth, to smell the cooking fat on his clothes. I avoided eye contact: common sense, don't challenge him.

'Those glasses are well sad, you look like Elton John, anybody ever tell you that?'

'Let me past,' I said, 'or I'll report you to the police.'

'Yeah,' he raised an eyebrow, 'got a mobile phone in there have you?' He made a grab for the sports bag. I swung it backwards out of his reach.

Mr Poole's door swung open and light spilt across the path. 'What's going on?' he barked. There were two women close behind him in the doorway.

'Aw, fuck off, grandad,' yelled the boy who I'd not seen before.

'Clear off,' shouted Mr Poole, 'go on, clear off. We're sick of the lot of you.'

'You should be ashamed of yourselves,' one of the women spoke up.

Catcalls and clapping. The twin inched out of my way. Mickey Whittaker gave us two fingers.

I hurried into the house. Mr Poole shut the door. There was a hard thump from outside. It made me start.

'Football,' said Mr Poole, 'they've been kicking it over the road against the door for the last ten minutes.' He closed his eyes momentarily, shook his head. 'Are you alright?'

'Yes, I'm OK.' But raging inside.

'This is Mary,' he introduced the woman who'd called out. She was small, energetic, bright-eyes and a quick smile. We shook hands.

'And Pauline.'

Pauline's hand was cool and frail, everything about her looked pale, faded.

'We're his secretaries,' joked Mary, 'help him sort his files out.'

'More like gaffers,' he joked, 'keep me on my toes. Local history buffs,' he explained, 'know all about Hulme, these two do.'

The women both grinned.

'I'd better get going,' I gestured upstairs.

'We'll get you a brew. Tea?'

'Thank you.'

'They know what you're doing,' Mr Poole said to me.

'It's not all like this, you know,' Mary tapped my arm. 'You look in the paper and it's all "estate from hell" and "crime and despair" but there's some good people round here, proper little communities. This side of the road, we've not had all the changes they have over there.'

'We're not the New Hulme,' added Pauline, 'they've knocked that down twice in my lifetime. St Georges has had a different history. Lot more settled.'

'Thought we'd died and gone to heaven when we moved here, didn't we Pauline?'

'Oh, aye. We was all moved from the slums, see. Beswick and Salford. You'll not remember but they was terrible places, really terrible. We came here and there's indoor toilets – cos we only had a privvy in the yard before that.'

'Hot water out the tap and all,' added Mary, 'I cried the first time I saw that. Tears of joy.'

'She does exaggerate,' teased Mr Poole. Mary slapped him on the arm.

'You go on up,' he said, 'I'll bring your tea up.'

I opened the window a couple of inches then set the camera up as before. I was smarting with outrage at the bullying I'd had to deal with. I knew I'd done right to play cautious, to save my skin but I had been in many similar situations and every time there was a small part of me, enraged at the injustice of it, at the brutal cocksure arrogance of these men (for they always had been men) and each time I had swallowed that anger. One day, I fantasised, I'd let go, let all that rage free, let it come pouring out and I'd kill someone, batter them to death with whatever was to hand, strangle them with my bare hands, beat them to a pulp … and more. And then how would I feel? Better?

I checked the focus, I couldn't see the lads at all then I realised that they must be leaning against the van parked directly outside the house. The football would appear now and then and they began to target the Ibrahims' house, kicking the ball hard against the door and windows. I couldn't film them but I took some footage of the ball to establish what was happening.

Mr Poole brought me some tea. 'I thought what had happened on Friday would be enough to convince the council.'

'It may be but they're waiting for the lawyer's say-so.'

He grunted, not impressed and told me to call him if I needed anything.

I looked back at the house opposite. The football slammed against the door and bounced back. How did the Ibrahim children react to the bombardment? Could they sleep? Did they have nightmares and wet the bed? Did they huddle under the covers trying to shut out the noise? What would Mrs Ahmed do? Try and keep life normal: bedtime now, brush your teeth, I'll tell you a story. Or did she gather them all together, ready for another night's siege, snuggled on the sofa with the video turned up loud playing the Lion King or Jungle Book.

After five minutes or so a man came from the bottom of the road, climbed into the van and drove off. I zoomed in and got a head shot of each of the twins. I couldn't tell them apart; only different coloured sweatshirts marked one from the other. Black and red. I panned round to take in Micky Whittaker with the bulldog tattoo on his skull and the fourth boy who wore a Manchester United cap backwards and had a close cropped beard on his chin. None of the boys wore coats in spite of the incessant drizzle.

The kicking continued, they concentrated on the lounge window. Thump, thump, thump. They took turns to kick, keeping the rhythm up like footballers in training. At last a powerful kick from Micky Whittaker smashed the window. I filmed their jubilation as they leapt into each others' arms and crowded round Whittaker. There was no sign of anyone inside the house. I used my mobile phone to call the police.

I reported malicious damage and threatening behaviour. I gave the location and my name. I pulled back the zoom till I had a general view of the scene and left the camera running.

Mr Poole was already opening the front door as I came downstairs. Mary and Pauline were in the hall in their hats and coats.

'They've smashed the window,' I told him, 'I've called the police.'

The group were by the gate lighting cigarettes.

'What do you think you're playing at?' Mr Poole demanded. 'The council can take you to court for breaking stuff like that.'

'Oooh, I'm scared,' minced Whittaker. 'Not.'

'They're not gonna do 'owt for a fuckin'

broken winder, are they?' One of the twins spoke.

'Was an accident, anyway,' his brother added.

A gust of wind stirred the curtains opposite.

'Clear off,' shouted Mr Poole, his voice rich with fury, 'clear off.' His jowls shuddered as he yelled. 'You've done enough damage.'

A few curses then the group began to play with the ball in the middle of the street.

'Shocking,' said Pauline, 'brass-necked cheek, they've no decency.'

Mr Poole turned away. 'I'll ring emergency repairs,' he said, 'they'll need that boarding up tonight.' He went through to his phone.

I went back to the doorway and stood there staring at the gang while they had their kickabout. I hoped to discomfort them. There was little reaction though I caught a few obscenities which I was sure were for my benefit. There was no sign of the police.

A private hire car came down from the main road and tooted at the boys who took their time to edge out of the way. The car drove down the Close to turn and drew up outside Mr Poole's. 'There's a taxi here,' I called.

'That's ours. Be seeing you Frank.' The women came to the door.

'I'd ring the police again you know,' said Mary, 'they don't always come unless you pester them.'

They said goodbye and walked slowly to their taxi.

Mr Poole came back out. 'They shouldn't be long, the repairs.'

'I thought they always took forever.'

'Not the emergencies. It's the rest that's a problem. They'll board that up tonight but it might be months before they get round to replacing the glass.'

'Mary said I should ring the police again.'

He nodded. 'Can't hurt.'

I dialled and got put through to the same man.

'I rang fifteen minutes ago and no-one's arrived yet.'

'They should be there soon, there's no immediate danger is there? Things haven't escalated?'

'Well, no.'

The lads were heading the ball now. Still outside the Ibrahims' but not directing their attention at their victims at present.

'It's a volatile situation though.' I said. 'The people in the house must be absolutely petrified. There's children in there. The police need to move these youths away before they do anything else.'

'There's a car in the area,' he said, 'should be with you soon.'

By my watch it took a further seventeen minutes before the white squad car appeared. During that time the Brennan twins nipped down home for some cans of lager and brought them back along with a large spliff which the four of them shared. When the car came into view the lads moved closer together on the opposite pavement. The car stopped beside them and the two occupants, a man and a woman got out. I couldn't hear what was being said but it seemed very light-hearted. The twins were grinning and at one point the whole group laughed aloud. The police turned away and crossed over to join Mr Poole and I by his gate.

'Mr Poole.' The man was older than Carl Benson, the policeman who'd come out the previous time, he moved languidly as though he was experiencing gravity differently from the rest of us. 'Miss Kilkenny.' He nodded at me. 'PC Doyle.' He turned his head slowly to the woman at his side, 'WPC Gilmartin. You reported the incident?'

He was grinning nearly all the time, nodding his head to some slow beat. He reminded me of a Jack Nicholson character, all lazy amusement and hidden menace. I wondered if he were stoned, his eyes were glassy, lids drooping a bit. Maybe he'd had a long shift.

'Seems like a little horseplay got out of hand. I've had a word with the lads and…'

'Hang about,' interrupted Mr Poole, 'it's not horseplay. This lot are terrorising that family. The council and the police know all about it. Your lot have been called out here countless times these last few weeks.'

He went on to outline all the forms the harassment had taken. PC Doyle didn't like being corrected. The grin faded, was replaced by a pained frown and he looked to the sky while Mr Poole spoke. A belittling gesture. His colleague was doing her best to be invisible. She neither spoke nor even watched what was going on. Feet close together, eyes down, she rocked now and again lightly on her heels and waited.

When Mr Poole finished Doyle grinned again. 'I've made a note of the incident, it's been recorded.'

'Aren't you going to see Mrs Ahmed?' I demanded. 'Reassure her?'

'Mrs Ahmed?' He gave a little extra weight to the name, very subtle but enough to signal that he was a bigot too. 'Mrs Ahmed doesn't speak any English.'

'I still think you should show her you're here. We can tell her the window will be boarded up tonight.'

He sighed. His eyes flicked to me then away. They looked hard, reptilian. He turned and walked in a slow roll over to the house followed at a distance by the WPC, Mr Poole and myself. The gang still hovered round the gateway. Why hadn't he sent them away? He banged on the door hard four times and shouted 'Police.' He sounded like he was going to launch a raid on the place not reassure a frightened citizen. There was no response. Surprise, surprise.

I went up to join him. As I passed the youths one of them made sucking noises.

PC Doyle banged again. 'Police.'

I spoke too. Maybe a woman's voice would be less threatening. After all how did Mrs Ahmed know whether this wasn't yet more aggro from the gang, a trap to get her to open the door?

'Mrs Ahmed,' I said, 'my name's Sal, I'm staying with Mr Poole, are you alright? Will you open the door?'

I waited for a minute then repeated it. Mr Poole, at my elbow, called out too. 'It's Mr Poole – the police are here and we're going to get the window fixed.'

'She doesn't speak English,' PC Doyle rolled his eyes at our stupidity, 'there's no point in trying to talk to her.'

'The children will though,' I retorted. 'One of them's at school, they'll probably be used to translating for her.'

He looked affronted.

I knocked again, gently. 'Mrs Ahmed, please open the door.' There was the sound of bolts being drawn back and then the door opened a crack. She kept the chain on. She stood there, five foot nothing, face still, scarf over her hair. Her eyes glanced rapidly over us all. At her side a small boy, Tom's age I guessed, in faded Batman pyjamas.

I spoke to him. 'Please tell your mother that Mr Poole has called someone to come and fix the window tonight.'

'From the council,' added Mr Poole.

The boy spoke to his mother. She inclined her head once. Her expression didn't change.

'The police are here and we hope these people will go to court very soon.' I waited while he passed on my words. 'They will be told to leave you alone or they will lose their houses and have to leave the area or maybe go to prison.'

She listened to her son then glanced at me. There was no hope in the look she gave me, just blank indifference. She didn't believe a word of it, she couldn't imagine it happening. Words meant nothing. Only actions, only when the victimisation stopped would our promises have meaning.

'I'm staying at Mr Poole's,' I repeated, 'I'll be there till your husband gets back. If there's anything I can do let me know.' The boy translated.

An empty offer really but I hoped that she would understand that I would be watching out.

'PC Doyle is going to send the boys home now – he'll come back if there's any more trouble. Goodnight.'

The child nodded and shut the door. Doyle smiled at me, angry and boxed in by my statement. If he didn't do it he'd compromise his authority – we might suspect he couldn't handle the teenagers. If he refused I was pretty sure I could register an official complaint about his conduct – though it probably wouldn't be pursued beyond a quiet reprimand.

He strolled down to the gate and spoke quietly to the boys. Eyes flicked my way. There was a burst of laughter and then the lads shambled away. The overwhelming impression was of a bunch of people in cahoots not that of an officer of the law dealing with law-breakers.

Mr Poole explained it to me as I made a drink in his kitchen. 'He's the one I told you about, bad penny. Agrees with that lot,' he said contemptuously.

'Gave me the creeps. And the police-woman never said a word.'

'Doesn't dare, he's the boss. He's probably giving her a hard time of it already.'

I poured water into my mug, stirred the coffee.

'With tonight as well,' I said, 'they should have enough to go to court, they must have.'

He moved to a kitchen chair, lowering himself cautiously to sit down. 'I suppose they need to have a watertight case,' he said, 'make sure they've dotted the i's and crossed the t's, it's only right that you've got to have good grounds to take someone's home away but even so when you see how they behave…'

'She looked so … hopeless,' I said, 'depressed. And there's two other children?'

'Aye, a baby few months old and a toddler. Little lad's at school. I see her taking him up there, others in the trolley.'

'What about Mr Ibrahim?'

'He's quiet, friendly enough considering. He was a teacher before the war – schoolteacher. He speaks a fair bit of English. I showed him the archives,' he gestured towards the back room. 'He was interested in that.'

We contemplated their savage change of circumstances. I sipped at my coffee. 'I'll take this up.'

'I doubt that they'll be back tonight. Pubs shut a while ago and there's no sign of the men.'

At midnight a van arrived and fixed a sheet of plywood to the broken window. After they'd left the man I'd seen before walked his dog along the Close and waited while it crapped on the pavement. I filmed them just for the hell of it. At one fifteen a cacophony of fire engine sirens rent the air, whooping past on the main road. At two thirty five Mr Ibrahim returned in a taxi. I saw him stop for a moment when he saw the boarded up window then hurry up the drive. Maybe I should have rung him at work and warned him about it but I hadn't got the number. I thought about going over to ask him for it but all being well this would be my last stint on Canterbury Close. It was late, I was knackered and I was sure the Ibrahims could do without any more callers.

Mr Poole was dozing in the lounge, I didn't wake him. I pulled the door to behind me. It was cold but at last the drizzle had stopped. The wet had brought out the smells of the gardens, soil and rotting leaves, the tarmac and concrete. I walked down to my car. My stomach did a somersault, my mouth soured. Aw, shit. The bastards had nicked my car.

Chapter Eleven

I reported the theft to the police on my mobile and rang a taxi. I sat on the low wall in front of Mr Poole's to wait. The wig was driving me mad and I'd a headache starting. I wondered whether to ring Ray but decided against it – there was no point in waking him just to say I'd be half an hour later than expected.

It was quiet on the Close. I could hear occasional traffic from the main road. My eyes felt hot and itchy, my back stiff from the tension and from peering into the viewer in the camera. I was ravenous too. Most nights I went to bed by eleven; my body was confused at being up hours after. It wanted breakfast.

The taxi arrived and hooted loudly as it rolled down the Close, pretty inconsiderate I thought given the time of night.

I waved and he sped to the bottom, circled round and roared back up to where I was waiting. Asian boy racer.

Once inside I gave him my address in Withington. 'Go down the Parkway, yeah?'

'Fine.' The dual carriageway had a higher speed limit which would suit his driving style and get me home quicker.

I settled back into my seat, leopard print suedette covers, a pair of pink fun fur elephants dangling from the rear-view mirror along with his i.d., V. Chowdury. Did he choose to have the car tarted up like this? Was it meant to be ironic?

We drove through the New Hulme; a huge development initiative that had replaced the massive Crescents, curving high rises and the nearby deck-access blocks with human-sized housing. I could see the graceful line of the Hulme Arch, over Princess Road, a symbol of optimism. Like Pauline had said this was the second attempt to renovate the area. Would it work? The houses looked nice enough, there had been a huge consultation exercise with the communities in the area as part of the project. They'd knocked down the old buildings but how would they get rid of the poverty, nestling like mould, spores ready to bloom and start the process of disintegration all over again?

I pulled the wig off, delighted to be rid of it. I rubbed at my head and the back of my neck. The driver did a double take in the mirror. Opened his mouth and shut it again.

A bit later. 'Been waiting long?'

'No, my car's been nicked.'

'Left it round there?'

'Yeah.'

'Have the shirt off your back round there, you know. You see that documentary the other night? Car crime capital of Europe, Manchester is. They ship some of them across to Russia, Ladas and that. Others they do a make-over drive them down to Brum or over to Liverpool. Lot of money in it. A mate of mine, he's parked outside the Palace, on Oxford Street, right, got a cab like…'

I switched off and gripped the edge of my seat as he cornered the junction onto Princess Parkway. I grunted now and then while he regaled me with stories of auto-theft. The narrative was seamless, one anecdote rolling into the next. When I did tune in again I noticed he'd an amazing eye for detail. 'So she says, "it's OK, I left the shopping in the boot," Marks and Sparks were doing a special offer on ready meals for one and she'd stocked up like. Now, she doesn't eat meat but she's mad on fish so there's all these heat-and-eat dinners going off and the police thought they'd got a body in the boot…'

Home at last.

'So what do you do?' he asked as I fished out my purse.

'I'm a private investigator.'

He laughed.

I looked at him.

'What, you're not winding me up?'

I pulled out one of my cards and passed it to him.

'Bloody 'ell,' he said.

I gave him a tenner.

'So what do you do, missing persons and that?' He rummaged for change in a little bag.

I thought of Jennifer Pickering. 'Yeah, that sort of thing.'

'Not missing cars though, eh?' he cackled.

'Ha, ha.' Rapier-like wit.

'Security and that, CCTV, bugs?'

'No, I don't do much of the high tech stuff.'

He handed me my change and I tipped him.

'Ta. See, I've got a mate who might be interested in this,' he waved my card. 'His old man's done a bunk. That the sort of thing you do?'

'Yes.' He still seemed to doubt me, his eyes flicked me up and down. 'What's with the wig then?'

I leant forward. 'I'm in disguise,' I confided and removed the specs. 'I don't usually dress like this.'

He laughed with relief. 'Had me worried then,' he shook his head, 'those glasses.'

Those seat covers.

We said goodnight. I could imagine I would become a new addition to his stock of city tales. 'I picked up this woman right, grey hair, painful glasses…'

Digger the dog greeted me at the door, had a sniff of my mac and sloped off, tail wagging slowly, back to sleep in the kitchen.

What would happen to Digger if Ray moved out? I felt a rush of panic. Ray adored the dog although I'd actually brought him home in a fit of guilt after his owner had died while helping me on a case. I'd quickly realised I was not a doggy person but Ray came to the rescue. It would be awful if Ray left Digger here with me, the dog would pine away. And if he took Digger, Maddie would lose a beloved pet as well as Tom and Ray. I couldn't think it through then, I was bone tired. I needed something to eat or I'd sleep badly. I made some quick porridge, smothered it in golden syrup and stirred in some thick Greek yoghurt. Perfect.

I was upstairs in the bathroom, brushing my teeth when Maddie cried out. I went in to her.

'There was a thing, Mummy, in my dream.' She was sitting bolt upright, her face crinkled with anxiety. I sat beside her and put my arm around her.

'What sort of a thing?'

'Horrible.' Her voice wobbled.

'Do you want to tell me your dream?'

She shook her head emphatically.

'OK, lie down then.'

She began to protest.

'It won't come back,' I said, 'it's only a dream, a picture in your sleep.' She wasn't having it, her mouth pulled ready for tears.

'Maybe you could put your tape on,' I suggested.

She paused, considering. 'Will you stay?'

I sighed.

'Just a bit Mummy and then leave the tape on?'

'Alright. I'll just get changed.'

She leaped out of bed. No way was she going to stay alone in the room after that thing had been in her dream. She shadowed me to my room and back.

I settled her in, stuck the story tape in the machine and sat back in the rocking chair. Tom in the other bed slept undisturbed. Maddie mouthed the words to the story. I closed my eyes. When I opened them again she was asleep and the tape had finished. I padded across the landing and fell into bed. And then it was time to get up again.

When I don't get enough sleep my concentration goes to pot. I knew I was going to spend the whole of Tuesday in a fuzzy state.

I had a big breakfast to compensate; half a grapefruit, mushrooms and scrambled egg, toast and honey. I dragged Maddie and Tom away from the telly and got them to school, went to my office straight from there. I made a coffee and drank it with my eyes closed and feet up before I attempted any work. I made a list of things I had to do in the course of the day. Then I considered my appointments. I'd a meeting with Frances Delaney at ten thirty and I was seeing Roger Pickering later to give him the low-down on what I'd discovered. That would take all of five minutes, I thought in my disgruntled mood. I pulled out the report I'd started and glanced over it. Alright, I reasoned with myself, maybe you haven't found Jennifer yet but you've established some facts that Roger wasn't sure of. I counted them off on my fingers. One – she was pregnant, two – Maxwell was the father, three – she left for university a week before the starting date, four – her friends were surprised at her sudden departure...

I was interrupted by the sound of footsteps up the path. I stood and craned my neck – caught sight of a Royal Mail uniform through the narrow basement window. I heard the clang of the letterbox and went up to check the mail. Most of it was for the Dobsons, I left it on the hall table, but there was also something for me. Brown, window envelope postmarked Keele. Yes! I hurried back downstairs, opening it as I went.

'Dear Ms Kilkenny,

Further to your recent enquiry concerning Jennifer Louise Pickering, 4.3.58, I have checked university records for the academic year 1976-77. Miss Pickering accepted a place for that year, conditional on her A-level grades, but she did not register for admittance. She was not a student of the English Faculty, or of any other University department, during that period.

Yours faithfully,

Mrs V. Halliday (Administrator)'

What?
I read it twice. Then I rang Mrs Halliday.

Chapter Twelve

I introduced myself and thanked her for the letter. 'I wanted to ask, registering for admittance – is that what students do when they actually arrive, during Fresher's Week?'

She expelled air quickly, sounding frustrated with my question. 'Yes,' she said brusquely, 'we have to keep track of numbers obviously, and if someone had been through admissions and joined the Faculty they would be on the general register.'

'What if she'd been admitted but dropped out of the course early on?'

'Then there would be a record of admission.'

'Do you know if Jennifer contacted the university to say she wasn't going to take her place?'

I heard her tut in exasperation. 'No. And that sort of documentation wouldn't have been kept as a matter of course. Our records weren't computerised until the mid-eighties, space was at a premium, official records were all we could find room for and there are boxes full of those, I can tell you.'

'And you checked for other departments as well?'

'According to the formal admissions records Jennifer Pickering did not attend this university at all.'

I was stunned. Everything had been resting on Keele. Jennifer's last known residence. Except it hadn't been. I'd hoped to find a firm lead there, a forwarding address, perhaps the names of course mates who might still be in touch. I made another coffee and tried to work out what this meant. Jennifer never went to Keele. Everyone assumed that she had. There was more to it than that. I dug out my earlier notes and went back over them. Both Roger and Mrs Clerkenwell had spoken about Jennifer dropping out of her course, so had Lisa MacNeice. And who had told them that Jennifer had left Keele? Mrs Pickering – Jennifer's mother. And who had told Mrs Pickering? Had Jennifer pretended to be at Keele when she was really elsewhere? Or had the Pickerings invented the story for reasons of their own? I had to talk to her. She must be able to tell me more about where Jennifer went at the end of that hot, dry summer. When I saw Roger later that day I would insist on meeting Mrs Pickering as a condition of carrying on with the case.

I looked at the letter again and tried to adjust my view of events to fit. I must erase the part about Jennifer going off to university. Why hadn't she gone? Her grades were good, people said she was excited about the move away, looking forward to it by all accounts. The pregnancy must have changed things. Did this mean she hadn't had an abortion but had decided to keep the baby, or at least continue the pregnancy? Where had Jennifer gone if not to Keele? To a mother and baby home? Couldn't she have deferred her course for a year while she had the baby?

I picked up the little mosaic vase that Mrs Clerkenwell had given me and turned it to and fro, examining the tiny fragments of glass mosaic the glinting gold pieces, the irregular colours of the small tiles. It felt cool to the touch. Together the broken pieces made something whole thanks to the craft of its maker. My work felt like that, lots of bits that needed matching together; facts, secrets, hearsay, rumours, all needed fixing in the right place, juxtaposing with the others until the true shape could be discerned. I was recreating truth not beauty. And truth could be hideous or poignant or whimsical or mundane.

I felt uneasy about the job. It had been hard enough at the outset with so many years since anyone had seen Jennifer but now to find that one of the few facts I had to work with was false made it feel even more of a lost cause. I shivered. The office suddenly felt small, cold and confining.

I rubbed my eyes, got up and switched on the heater, looked at the list I'd made first thing. Tell insurance, borrow car. Who from? Diane didn't have a car, she roped me in every time she had to transport frames or canvases or collect new tubs of inks and chemicals. Ray hadn't got one at the moment, he borrowed mine too and more recently made use of Laura's. Everyone I could think of who had a car actually used it and wouldn't be prepared to lend it out. I thought about the next few days. Most of my appointments could be done by bicycle. I should be able to manage. If Mr Poole rang again I'd get a taxi.

That reminded me to get the tape off to Mandy Bellows. I'd brought it to the office. I replayed a section of it in the camera to check that it was reasonable quality. It was.

I could make out the individuals, cocky faces sneering as they took turns to ram the ball against the house. I packed the tape in a jiffy bag and rang the courier service I use.

Then I rang the insurers and began the long, slow process of giving them all the details they needed about my stolen car.

Once the courier had called I got ready to leave. There was a noise upstairs, someone coming in. Unusual, as Grant and Jackie Dobson are teachers and rarely home when I am there, and their daughters are at school.

I went upstairs quietly, feeling foolish at how hard my heart was beating. There was someone in the kitchen. I positioned myself near the front door before calling out, 'Hello?'

'Sal?' a husky voice replied and Vicky Dobson, the eldest daughter, popped her head round the door. 'Hiya. I've just got back. Don't come too near, I need a bath, seriously.' Vicky had been doing the festivals; Glastonbury, Reading, WOMAD and had gone backpacking round Europe in-between. She looked the part; muddy blonde dreadlocks, a set of rings in each nostril, enough in her ears to hang curtains on, a stud in her eyebrow, distressed clothing, acid green Doc Martens. She looked great.

'Good trip?'

'Top. I'm knackered. And starving. I must eat – you want anything?'

'No, I've got to get going. See you soon.'

Frances Delaney had a baby draped over her shoulder when she answered the door. 'Typical,' she said, 'he always sleeps at this time, until I arrange something. Come in.'

'Don't worry,' I said, 'mine was just the same.'

'How many have you got?'

'Oh, only the one of my own but we share a house so there's a little boy as well.'

'I've four,' she said, 'well, four at the moment.'

'You're having another?'

She smiled. 'I always wanted a big family, sometimes you get what you want.'

We sat in a large room, strewn with baby gear and children's toys. There was a distinct smell to indicate she'd just changed a nappy. She wore a shapeless, navy jogging suit and moccasin slippers. Her dark wiry hair was pulled back in a yellow hair band. The baby wriggled on her shoulder, she rocked and patted its bottom. She looked ridiculously happy.

I asked her to tell me about the weeks before Jennifer left. I wouldn't let on to Frances that Jennifer had never gone to Keele; it was my job to find things out not divulge them. Roger Pickering was paying my way and any information belonged to him first and foremost.

'I remember it well, actually, with it being so hot. It was incredible, everything drying up. We used to watch her father watering his plants, every night after work he'd be out there.'

Like my Dad with his vegetables.

'You watched him?' I was trying to picture where the girls had been.

'From my room, it overlooked the gardens. Jenny would come round a lot, our house was right at the back of theirs. We could see across to each others' bedrooms.' The baby grizzled and made climbing motions, the stretch fabric of the baby-gro outlining his small limbs and feet. Frances shifted him onto her lap, laid him across her knees on his stomach and stroked his back. His head bobbed like those nodding dogs people used to have in the back window of their cars.

'Jenny would come over through the back,

169

climb over the wall and come in our back door. We even had a code,' she laughed, 'if I was going out I'd close my curtains so she'd know not to call.'

'She always came to yours?'

'Yes, her family were pretty old fashioned, it was easier at mine,' she shrugged. 'That summer Jenny was working up at The Bounty and I was just messing about. I'd got a place at Manchester University. Jenny and Lisa went off to Knebworth, I don't know why I didn't go, short of cash I suppose. I went up to the Lakes with my family for a week. When I got back Jenny came over. She told me about the baby.' She looked at me to check my reaction, had I known? I nodded, it wasn't news to me.

'Did she say whether she was going to keep it?'

She shook her head, her expression clouded. 'We didn't talk about it much. I was pretty anti-abortion then, Jenny knew that. We had a lot of visits from LIFE at my school, gory slide shows.' She sighed. 'So, I told her places she could go, have the baby adopted, but she was very mixed up. After that we skirted round it, really. I was pretty blinkered back then. You know how teenagers can be, everything's black and white, we all think we know it all. I think I've mellowed since then, I hope so. When I got to university I got involved in the Catholic Feminist Society.'

Something of a contradiction in terms I thought to myself.

'It was all very radical, certainly opened my eyes. We wanted to reform the position of women in the Church and challenge a lot of the dogma. I suppose my position changed but I never saw Jenny again.'

'Can you remember the last time you saw her?'

The baby wailed, a loud, harsh cry as though the world had suddenly ended. 'Shush, shush, come here,' she turned him over, cradled his head and body in one arm while she lifted the corner of her top with the other and slipped him onto her breast. 'You'd think he hadn't had a feed for hours,' she commented. The baby was quiet immediately.

I had a flash of memory of the sensation of breast-feeding, breasts tender and heavy with milk, the initial buzz almost painful as Maddie latched on, the relief as she sucked, the other nipple leaking in sympathy. I'd had my share of problems, two bouts of mastitis when it felt as though someone had poured hot concrete laced with acid into my breast but apart from that I'd loved it.

'I couldn't tell you what day it was, or anything, but I remember it because Jenny got upset and I wasn't sure if I'd said something, you know, something stupid...'

'Go on,' I encouraged her.

'We'd been in my room, it was early evening but it was still hot. My room was stifling and we decided to go out in the garden. I got a rug and the radio, pop, that sort of thing.' She stroked the baby's legs and squeezed his feet all the time she was talking. 'Jenny was a bit low really, most of the time she was so sparky, tons of energy but she was on edge. I probably did most of the talking. It got late and she was all ready to go. She climbed up the wall and then she came back. I thought she'd forgotten something but she pushed past me and went off down the side. I ran after her, asked what was wrong, she rounded on me, told me to leave her alone, said I'd no idea – something like that. She was crying. I felt awful.' She chewed at her lip. 'I tried ringing later but the phone was engaged.'

'What do you think upset her?'

'I don't know, something I'd said, maybe me prattling on when she was so worried?

There was I lounging around not a care in the world, and she's pregnant and confused. Plus she can't even confide in me because she knows how I feel about abortion. Or maybe it was the thought of going home, maybe she just couldn't face them.'

'Had she told her parents she was pregnant?'

'No, I don't think so. Lisa said that Jenny wanted to decide what she was going to do before she said anything. So she'd stormed off and I phoned the next day, it was Caroline's birthday do, we were going to go into town together, but there was no answer. I felt awful. I thought Jenny had not come because she was cross with me. I got horribly drunk. I did try to ring a couple of times after that then when I finally did get through her mother said she'd gone to Keele. I couldn't believe it. I rang Lisa and she told me it was true.'

'Why was it hard to believe?'

'She never said goodbye – not even to Lisa. And she never took her mascot, it was still on her windowsill – that's why I thought she was still at home. We all had them, little troll things, peculiar really. We took them into exams for good luck. Jenny had kitted hers out in this glam rock outfit and drawn

173

make up on it.'

I felt an unpleasant undertow of apprehension. It didn't add up. Jennifer had been a gregarious teenager with a circle of close friends. She'd left without so much as a goodbye. Without her lucky mascot. None of them had ever heard from her. She hadn't even sent her little brother a birthday card on the day they shared. Had she run away? Had something happened to her that meant she couldn't keep in touch with her friends?

My imagination conjured up new pictures, Jennifer on the run. Lost in London. Hurt. Worse. I was being melodramatic, I told myself. There must be a simple explanation. But a seed of suspicion had taken root. I kept coming back to the explanation that fit everything so far. If Jennifer Pickering was dead then it all made sense.

Chapter Thirteen

I left Frances Delaney, thanking her for her time. It was another balmy autumn day, the warm sunshine and soft air at odds with the gripe in my stomach and the tension in my neck. I needed to unwind a little, think things through before my one o'clock appointment.

I cycled home and took refuge in the garden. Several large trees frame the space, their leaves were turning and many were scattered across the grass. I sat in the sun with my pen and paper, a bowl of carrot and red pepper soup. Insects and floating seeds drifted in the air, spider webs glinted on the clematis and across the kitchen windows. I drank my soup and let the snippets of information jostle in my mind for a while, then I wrote down a list of what I knew followed by what I suspected. I had no proof that Jennifer was dead. After all she might have just cut everything and everyone off, started a new life and never looked back. People do. There are hundreds of people who just walk out of their lives into new ones, leaving families to tear themselves apart with worry and pain.

A squirrel raced along the wall at the bottom of the garden, paused and sat on its haunches, then scampered back up the tree in the corner. Jennifer Pickering had been on the brink of returning home, half-way over the wall, when she'd become upset. Thinking perhaps about her parents and the baby and how everything was going off the rails. The stifling atmosphere that awaited her even before she told them about her pregnancy. Did she run away then, leaving her precious troll behind?

I'd have to keep on searching for more clues as to what had become of her. Roger might ask me to drop the case then what chance would I have to prove my suspicions either way? I didn't want to give up. Even with so little to go on I was determined to try everything I could think of to find out what had befallen Jennifer Pickering. My intuition told me that I wouldn't find Jennifer alive – but I had been wrong before. Maybe I just wouldn't find her at all.

I wrote down what further enquiries I could make if Roger Pickering wanted me to carry on. High on the list was a talk with Mrs Pickering. Perhaps she could clear it all up. Had they bundled her off to some far flung relative for the duration? Could she come up with an old address for Jennifer, something she'd kept secret for all these years because her daughter had disgraced them by getting pregnant out of wedlock, by having a mixed-race child? Perhaps. Had she ever heard from her daughter? A car alarm shrieked, shattering the silence. I gathered up my things and got ready.

The office felt claustrophobic, the sun, low in the sky, streamed in the narrow window, spreading a wide beam in which the dust swirled. After banging a few times on the window frame I managed to open it and let some air circulate. I had my notes all ready, the kettle had boiled. I straightened the rug. I sat down again and stared at the blue abstract that Diane had done for me, letting different patterns and pictures emerge from the shapes of the inks. The bell rang. I went up and greeted Roger Pickering, escorted him down to my office. He didn't want a drink so I got straight down to business. 'First of all, there's your photo. I've had copies made so you can take that with you. Now, I've made notes of what I've done so far,' I began, 'I'll type them up for you and you'll have a copy to keep but I thought I should bring you up to date and discuss whether you want me to continue.'

'You've not found her?' He shook his fringe away from his eyes, his voice hesitant. Of course I hadn't. Did he really think I'd go through all the preamble if I'd success-fully traced his sister? It was hope that made him ask, I think, relentless optimism and the need to have his wildest dreams quashed before he could sensibly concentrate on anything else.

'No. And I'm not any nearer knowing where to look than I was last week. But I have established a few new facts. I heard from Keele University this morning.'

He glanced up keenly.

'She never went there, they have no record of her.'

He looked stupefied, even his mouth was open. 'But she was doing English...'

'I checked with the Faculty. She never attended.'

'I don't understand. My mother said...' he trailed off.

'I need to talk to your mother – she's the only person who can clear this up.'

He shook his head, slowly building up to a refusal.

'Let's come back to that. I have established a couple of other facts. First of all, Jennifer was pregnant.'

'Really,' his whole face lit up at the prospect.

'But she may not have had the child,' I cautioned him. 'Her friends say she was very unsure what to do; whether to go ahead or to have an abortion, whether to have the baby adopted or keep it.'

'You could check that though, couldn't you? If she had a baby there'd be a record of that, wouldn't there?'

'Yes.' And it would probably be easier to find than Jennifer was.

'I want you to find out,' his eagerness was poignant. I realised with a rush of understanding that Roger was re-inventing himself as an uncle, with nephew or niece to his name. Though they'd be in their mid-twenties by now.

'I'd have to go to Huddersfield,' I said, 'that's the nearest place with the most up to date national records. I don't think there's any point in going all the way to London. There is an office in Manchester too but they haven't got such a comprehensive archive.'

'Try Huddersfield then.'

'There's a problem, I've had my car stolen, I'll need to hire a car – for a day, add it to my expenses.'

'That's fine,' he said.

'I also found out who the father was. Someone that Jennifer met at the Bounty, the banqueting hall where she used to waitress. He's called Jones, Maxwell Jones. He's black and that probably made it even harder for Jennifer to confide in your parents.'

He gave me a puzzled look.

'Your father, in particular, held racist views.'

'Oh, yes,' he blushed.

'So not only had Jennifer broken faith with their moral and religious position she'd done so with someone your father could never accept.'

'Does he know? This man?'

'No. The relationship was over before Jennifer realised that she was pregnant. Her friends say she never considered marrying him, she knew she'd be on her own.'

He swallowed and covered his eyes briefly. 'It's a lot to take in.'

'Yes.' When he looked at me again I continued. 'We also know that no-one heard from Jennifer, none of her friends, and that they were surprised at her sudden departure.'

'But where can she have gone? If it wasn't Keele?'

'That's why I need to talk to your mother.'

'I don't think that's a good idea,' he protested. 'Did they know?' he asked quietly, 'about the baby, did my parents know?'

'I haven't been able to establish whether she told them or not.'

'What she said, my mother, about Jennifer being a disgrace, that must be what she meant.'

'Roger, I need to talk to your mother. She was the one who led everyone to believe Jennifer had gone to Keele and then dropped out, that's what she told Lisa and Mrs Clerkenwell and you. If anyone knows where she really went it's your mother.'

'I don't think she'll see you,' he stonewalled.

'Don't tell her.'

'What?'

'She'll be in this evening?'

'Yes.'

'I'll come round after you've eaten, I'll ask what I have to ask.'

He looked sick.

'The worst that can happen is that she'll throw me out.'

'And she'll know that I've hired you?'

'Yes. Look I could invent some mickey mouse story about being an old friend or a school re-union or something but all she's going to say is that she's lost touch with Jennifer. I have to challenge her, Roger.'

'She's not well.'

Was his concern for her or for himself? He was thirty one for heaven's sake, not a child. Wasn't it about time he stood up for himself? 'It's up to you,' I said tiring of his weakness, 'but if you won't give me a chance to talk to her I'm afraid I'm not prepared to carry on with the case.' I paused.

He stared at his hands as though they held the correct answer.

'Maybe she should know; that you've hired me, that you're determined to find your sister.'

'OK,' he sat back in the chair, 'come round about seven. She should still be awake – she has a room downstairs now, it's easier. Will I need to be there?'

'No. Just let me in and I'll see her on my own.'

A wave of doubt leapt at my conscience. Shouldn't I leave it all be, leave a dying woman to her secrets, let the mystery remain? I pressed my palms onto my desk to steady myself. I couldn't walk away from this. I was in too deep and I needed to know whether my intuition was playing me false, or whether Jennifer was dead rather than missing. And if she was dead was her death due to illness or accident or something more sinister? I had to find out and maybe then it would all come clear. It would all be right as rain, I would laugh at the disturbing fears that were multiplying in my imagination and the aching sensation in my stomach would melt away. Maybe.

A fine autumn evening, there was a fresh wind blowing, encouraging the trees to let go of their first dying leaves. The wind brought a cooler feel with it and I shivered as I pedalled along in spite of the heat generated by my cycling.

I leant the bike against the garage at the side of the house and locked the back wheel to the frame. It was exactly seven o'clock. I rang the bell and heard the shrill tone echo inside. Roger answered the door, his dread of my visit written all over his face. He lived with his mother in awe of her. Would he find release once she had gone? Shed his persona of nervous little boy?

'Come in, she's in here.'

The house was the mirror image of Mrs Clerkenwell's as far as its layout went, the front rooms off to the right of the passageway with the stairs at the left. The hall was dark, lots of deep polished wood, an antique umbrella and hat stand on the left. The floor was brown tiles with geometric border of blue and white triangles, a Victorian style. The kitchen door at the far end of the hall was ajar and through it spilt a ruby wedge of light from the setting sun. Like warmth in the distance. It didn't stretch the length of the hallway and when it suddenly faded everything was sombre and melancholy again.

I gestured for Roger to open the door and braced myself. I followed him in.

'There's someone to see you,' he said and withdrew.

She was sitting in a high-backed armchair, a crocheted rug over her legs and one of those v-shaped support pillows behind her. She looked haggard, her skin tone was yellow, she had a mob-cap on with lacy edge and I wondered whether the treatment had caused her hair to fall out. Her features were small, neat, and she wore bifocals on a chain. I could discern a slight resemblance to Jennifer in the thin nose and the small mouth but not to Roger who presumably took after his father. In her hands she held a little magazine, a puzzle book, full of crosswords and word-searches. She lay it down on her lap.

'Are you from The Children?'

'Pardon?'

'The Children of Christ?'

'No. Are you expecting someone?'

'Tomorrow, I think. They're very good.' Her voice was clear.

'You're still involved with the church?'

She stared at me for a moment. 'I am dedicated. The Children are my spiritual family, my one true family, surpassing all others. When all about is corruption'

She stopped. I don't know whether she was quoting something or making a social observation. I was still standing but there was nowhere for me to sit. A dining chair near to Mrs Pickering was covered in clothes and I didn't want to perch on the bed.

'No, I'm not from the church,' I said, 'I'm a private detective. I've come to talk to you about Jennifer.'

I thought she was going to keel over. Her eyes fluttered and she went even paler. She began to shake her head as though I were a noise she could dislodge.

'Jennifer has been missing since 1976,' I said. 'I'm trying to trace her.'

'Go away,' she said quickly, her mouth trembling.

'I'd like your help.'

'I don't know where she is, she went to university, after that I don't know.'

185

'She didn't go to Keele,' I said calmly, 'she never got there. That's what she had been planning to do, that's what you told people but it wasn't the truth.'

'Get out of here. Roger,' her voice rose, quavering.

I crouched down, better to talk to her at the same level. 'I know she was pregnant, did she tell you? It must have been a terrible shock.'

'Why are you asking me all this?' she cried, anguish in her voice.

'Roger wants me to find his sister, he wants it desperately enough to go against your wishes.'

'She went to Keele,' she repeated.

'She didn't, they've checked the records.'

'Roger,' she began to scream.

'Where did she really go?'

She got up and took a few steps still calling, 'Roger, Roger, Roger.'

'Did you ever hear from Jennifer?'

'Roger!'

The door flew open and Roger came in.

I stood up. I know when I've overstayed my welcome. 'I'll wait in the kitchen,' I said to him.

It was quarter of an hour before Roger joined me. I stared at the notice-board with its neat list of names and numbers, clinic appointment cards and money off coupons. I considered ways to get Mrs Pickering to talk to me but couldn't come up with anything that would get me past her hysteria. Why was she so agitated at the mention of Jennifer? Surely after twenty odd years the reaction to Jennifer's pregnancy would have softened a little? Jennifer must have told them about the baby, that much seemed evident. Was Mrs Pickering's illness affecting her emotional state? But according to Roger he'd had the same response a year previously.

I stared out of the back window to the house opposite where Frances Delaney had grown up and I worked out which had been her room. The stone wall separating the gardens was substantial, about six foot high, darkened by the smoke from the city before the Clean Air Act came in and they sandblasted everything.

When Frances talked about Jennifer climbing over the wall and becoming distraught I thought perhaps she'd been imagining what waited for her at home and it had all been too much. I re-considered. Could she have seen something? There was a large garden shed at the bottom of the

Pickering's garden and it would be about the only thing you'd see from the Delaney's wall. Had she seen something in the shed? I opened the door at the side of the kitchen and walked round to the back garden. It was uninspiring. Roger definitely hadn't inherited his father's green fingers. A couple of rhododendron bushes, some lavender and geraniums were all that stocked the borders, weeds were rampant in-between. The rest of the place was lawn, dotted with dandelions. I walked over to the shed and circled it, no windows. I went to the wall which was about four feet from the shed. I easily found foot holds in the stones and hoisted myself up until I was sitting on the top. A startled cat leapt down and shot away into the large trees at the bottom of the garden next-door. From my vantage point the shed obscured any view of the Pickering's house. I shuffled along to the left and found I could see the upper floors of Mrs Clerkenwell's. From the other end the house at the right, where the Shuttle's had lived was screened by a Leylandii hedge which grew above the dividing fencing. There was precious little chance of Jennifer seeing anything from there.

I made my way back to the kitchen.

Frances may have been right, something she had said had got to Jennifer or it was the thought of going home. But why so sudden? Had she made up her mind to tell them that evening and then panicked? And run away? Where? With no money, no spare clothes. As far as I could tell that had been the last that any of her friends had seen of her. She'd missed Caroline's birthday the following evening and no-one had seen hide nor hair of her since.

Suicide? I'd not thought of that. Her body never discovered? Or found but never identified? If she'd been anywhere in the Lancashire area it would have been all over the papers and the telly, her family or friends would have made a connection. But what if she'd gone to London or further afield, run out of hope there? Her parents had never reported her missing and it was doubtful whether Lisa's attempt to do so would have received much attention so if an unidentified body had been found they wouldn't have been able to compare dental records with those of missing persons.

It was all a mess, I thought, a hopeless, confusing mess. I rubbed my neck, trying to ease the tension lodged there. I heard Roger coming.

'Is she alright?'

'I think so. I've put her to bed. She's absolutely livid with me.'

I nodded. 'At least it's out in the open, now. She knows that you're serious. What do you think she'll do?'

'There's not much she can do. But she'll be difficult to live with. She's not used to me going against her.' He sighed and filled the kettle. 'Did she tell you anything?'

'No.' Just lies. 'Same old stuff about Jennifer going to Keele. Why do you think she's so upset?'

'I don't know, it's like I told you – she won't talk about it, like some ancient feud and I don't know what's behind it apart from Jennifer expecting the baby. But why she won't tell you, tell me…' he broke off in exasperation then sighed. 'Tea?'

'Coffee, if you've got it.'

Neither of us spoke until he'd made the drinks. He sat opposite me at the small table cradling the mug in his hands.

'Do you want me to carry on?'

'Yes.' He didn't need to think about it.

'Roger,' I wondered how to phrase it, 'I may not be able to find Jennifer, sometimes people just get lost, stay lost and with the time lapse…'

'I know,' he said. He cleared his throat. 'I want you to keep looking. I want you to go tomorrow. You said you could check the records to see if she had the baby.'

'Yes. There's something else to consider, too. You need to think about the possibility that Jennifer may no longer be alive.' The words sounded strained as I picked my way round the topic.

He paused for a beat, his body still. 'You can check that out too, can't you? When you go to Huddersfield?'

'Yes, I can, if her death was ever registered, if her identity was known. But her next of kin would have been notified unless there had been some mistake along the line. Another possibility is that Jennifer married and changed her name, she might never have told her husband she had any family, in that case he would have been her next of kin and your parents would never have been informed. So I'll look for marriages as well as the births and deaths.'

He swallowed. 'Right.' He looked at me then, his eyes glistening but his gaze steady. 'Because it would be better to know, whatever you find out, it would be better to know, wouldn't it?'

I had no answer.

Chapter Fourteen

I felt lousy cycling back from Roger's. The confrontation with Mrs Pickering had left a bitter taste in my mouth and the tension had given rise to a dull ache in my neck and shoulder. I admired Roger's determination that I should press ahead with my enquiries, especially after the fury of his mother, but I felt anxious at what I might find out. My hunch was that I would bring only bad news back from Huddersfield. I told myself it was his choice, he was a grown man, but it had hardly been a fully informed choice. Yes, I'd hinted at the possibility of Jennifer's death but I'd come nowhere near telling him I now thought that the most likely outcome.

I needed to work off some of the tension. I was pushing it for time but I just made it home to get towel and swimsuit and out again for the Tuesday night women only swim at Withington Baths. It was better going later, not so busy. I swam as fast as I could, pushing myself, feeling my legs tire and my lungs work hard. After thirty lengths

I walked up the steps, my legs wobbling from the exertion. I had a long shower, letting the water play on my sore shoulder. The water was hot but only stayed on for ten seconds at a time so I had to keep reaching up to press the knob again which made it hard to keep my back relaxed.

Ray and Laura were watching a video when I got back. I didn't feel like joining in. I asked Ray if he'd be able to collect Maddie and Tom from school the following afternoon. He mumbled a yes and snuggled closer to Laura who giggled at something. I wondered whether Laura had met Nana Tello yet. She'd be delighted at any sign of Ray getting ready to settle down properly with someone. She had always viewed our household and my presence as an awkward aberration which would stymie Ray's eligibility for romance and marriage and further grandchildren. I bet she was lighting candles to the patron saint of courtship on a regular basis.

Sheila was washing up in the kitchen; she shares it with us and has a flat in the attic with her own bathroom and sitting room.

'You look tired,' she said.

That made me yawn. 'I didn't get in till nearly three, my car got nicked last night.'

'Oh, no, where?'

I told her all about it as I made myself some tea and crumpets. 'And now,' I yawned, 'I'm absolutely shattered.'

'Early night?'

'Yes,' I didn't want to play gooseberry to the loving couple and I nearly said so to Sheila but it wasn't the right moment, really. If I was going to raise it we needed time for a good talk. I wanted to know if she found Ray had changed and what she thought about Tom and Ray leaving us or Laura moving in. 'What about you? Course going well?'

'I love it,' she laughed at herself. 'I've definitely got the bug. I'm hoping that they'll let me do a PHD after this.'

'Good for you.' She was in the second year of a degree course in geology, after the break up of a twenty-year marriage.

I slathered my crumpets with butter and Marmite and took them up with my drink. I read for a while but found it hard to concentrate. I checked on the kids before I went to bed. All was well. I had a bunch of late sweet-peas by my bed. I lay there and breathed in their perfume and tried not to think about work; about secrets and lies and snapshots of a girl with stars painted on her cheeks. I tried for ages. And then I slept.

The nearest car rental place was in Didsbury. I rang and checked that they could help me, then, armed with my driving licence, credit cards and proof of identity, I walked down there and got sorted out with a nice white Datsun. It had a stereo sound system which would help to relieve the tedium of the M62.

It was raining steadily as I drove out over Barton Bridge and got stuck in the queues for the massive Trafford Centre. The place had a wonderful dome but the prospect of miles of mall and hundreds of shops and shoppers was my idea of hell not heaven. If I ever had a few grand to spend it might be fun but even then I'd prefer wandering round real streets with sky above and proper city air and pigeons.

I reached the M62, peeling off from the traffic going west and began to climb the Pennine hills. Some are so steep there are crawler lanes for the heavy goods vehicles that have to slow down, but there were still plenty of manic trucks on the road that October day, slewing past me in a welter of spray and muck or travelling stubbornly in pairs, a lane each, vying to overtake. I was relieved to see the Huddersfield exit and content myself with getting lost in the one-way network.

The records of births, deaths and marriages were housed in the Local History Library. Once I'd found the right section I dutifully deposited my bag in one of the lockers. Pens were forbidden, presumably in case someone got carried away and scrawled 'found Grandma!' or 'this must be Harry's wife' on precious archives. I purchased a pencil and found a free microfiche viewer.

The place was quietly busy, to my left an elderly man was surrounded by papers and books which he referred to in between peering at his screen. To my right a young couple were working together and talking in whispers. The microfiches were kept in folders, each year divided into quarters. I went to the birth records folders and pulled out the one for 1977. I settled in front of the viewer, got my notebook and pencil ready and began to trawl through the entries.

Jennifer had been pregnant in the summer 1976, maybe only a few weeks but possibly two or three months, so I checked from the following spring through to autumn. There were three Pickerings; my heart leapt each time I saw the name – had I found Roger's niece or nephew? But when I examined the details each entry gave a different maiden name for the mother – these were women who had married a Pickering. I needed a Pickering whose maiden name was Pickering. No joy. If Jennifer had given birth there was no record of it.

Had she married? I repeated my search in the marriage records. Nothing. Steeling myself, I moved on to look at the Deaths. Beginning in 1976 I searched every year for Jennifer. There were two Jennifer Pickerings, but each was too old at seventy-seven and eighty-three to be the one I wanted. I finished the latest folders and sat back rolling my shoulders from the strain of peering at all the data. I needed a break from sitting scrolling through the lists so I retrieved my bag and went to get a coffee.

As I sipped it and munched on a flapjack I wondered whether there was anything else I could usefully do. There was no sign of Jennifer's death or of her baby's birth. Even if she had decided on adoption the original birth records would be here. Perhaps she had miscarried or gone for an abortion. She felt like a chimera. I'd seen her photograph, talked to her friends, met her family but she kept slipping through my fingers. Like she never existed.

It was instinct that made me return to the birth records again. I certainly had no clue what I was expecting to find. And the rational part of me thought I was just prevaricating because I didn't want to admit defeat and go home.

I got the folder for 1958. There was no Jennifer Pickering born in Manchester that year. There was no Jennifer Pickering born anywhere else either. I double checked. This was crazy.

'Yes!' The man to my left exclaimed, 'There's a marriage in York.' A couple of others stopped and smiled at his success.

I returned to the shelves and looked through the years either side, maybe Roger had got the year wrong. No luck. I was stumped. I sat and thought for a while. Go back a step, I told myself. Find the Pickerings' marriage. I didn't know Barbara's maiden name so I had to look for Frank. There was no entry for a marriage between a Frank Pickering and anyone in the three years before Jennifer was, supposedly, born. What was it with this family, where the hell were all their records? It was like the X-files or something.

I sat and tried to think it through. I drew

spirals on my notepad surrounded by question marks. I waited a while, thought some more. Where was Jennifer? Where was the marriage? Slowly, the penny chugged along the slope, lingered on the brink and then dropped. Was I right? I went through the microfiches. Yes! Pickering, Frank, married a woman, maiden name Carter, in Manchester in 1961. Jennifer would have been just over three years old at the time. I'd got it.

I felt a buzz of excitement as the new information raised fresh possibilities. Jennifer Pickering was illegitimate, born before the marriage. Well before. In all likelihood she wasn't Frank's child. But how come he had deigned to marry Barbara? She'd have been a fallen women in his eyes, surely? Jennifer had called him a hypocrite. Had she known about the details of her birth? Had she expected them to understand? Not according to her friends. Or had the fact of her illegitimacy only come out in the heat of the row which followed her announcement of her pregnancy, and then she'd rung Lisa, full of fury at the double standard. Her mother could be forgiven but she could not. But hang on, according to Lisa, Jennifer said her father's hypocrisy wasn't about her pregnancy. Was it about her mother's then? Had she needed papers for university and found out then that she was not Frank Pickering's child? Had she remembered all the sermons he had preached about the sanctity of marriage and the importance of purity, of fallen women and hellfires?

No wonder Barbara Pickering found it hard to talk about Jennifer; her daughter's pregnancy must have re-awakened all her buried feelings of disgrace and shame and revealed a secret that the family had jealously guarded. Had Jennifer demanded to know who her real father was? Whose blood ran in her veins? Could she have gone to him? Run away to find him cutting herself off from the family who had lied to her? My mind cartwheeled round the possible scenarios.

I pulled myself back to the task in hand, carefully noted the record and then went back to the birth records to find Jennifer Carter. When had they changed her name? Had they done it formally or was it just Pickering by usage? Would she have needed her birth certificate for anything? College? Passport? She had to be there. What would I do if she wasn't? My hand trembled a little as I slid the acetates into the glass holders. I peered at the screen, scrolled down to the surnames beginning with C. Oh, yes. There she was Carter, Jennifer. In the spring of 1958. Mother's maiden surname; Carter.

I didn't call out like my neighbour but I felt a glow of delight at unravelling the tangle. Then, because I pride myself on being thorough, I looked through all the records again to see if Jennifer had given birth, died or married using her original name of Jennifer Carter. Zilch.

It was way past lunchtime and my stomach was growling. The rain had stopped and I wandered about until I found a little curry house in the town centre and wolfed down a vegetable dansak and two chapattis. New questions about the case sprang up in my mind like cress on cotton wool. Had they ever told Jennifer that she wasn't Frank's biological daughter? Had she discovered the truth herself, coming upon the birth certificate, cheeks burning and guts revolving as the truth slapped her in the face? Wouldn't she have run to Lisa, though? Confided in her best friend? Around all my speculation circled the question that really mattered: where was Jennifer Pickering and was she dead or alive?

I tried to focus on the last few days before her disappearance. She had spoken to Lisa and she had been very upset; she'd called her father a hypocrite but when Lisa asked her if she'd told them about the baby, Jennifer said not. She'd been low at Frances's, (had that come sooner or later?) and then she had become distressed as she made to go home. Pushing her friend away, leave me alone. Sudden, it had been, as though she'd had a shock.

Then nothing. No-one had seen her, heard from her. And I'd talked to everyone I possibly could. I pulled out my original list. All except Mrs Shuttle who had slammed the phone down on me. Next door neighbour, moved to Bradford. Why so violent a reaction? What was behind it? It was only a few miles from Huddersfield to Bradford. I could pay an unexpected visit. What had I got to lose? An hour or so? I flipped back through my notebook looking for the phone number. I knew I'd written it down early on in my enquiries. Found it. I rang the number and a woman answered.

'Isabella?' I made my voice squeaky.

'You've got the wrong number.'

'Oops! Sorry.' Now don't go out before I

get there.

I bought an A-Z at the newsagents and worked out my route. They didn't live far from the motorway. As I rejoined the traffic I considered what questions to ask Mrs Shuttle. There would be little point in going over the same ground I'd covered with everyone else. I tried to come up with something other than 'why did you cut me off?' but I just couldn't concentrate. I was too distracted by the revelations of the records office. To be honest I hadn't got the foggiest what I'd say.

Chapter Fifteen

I left the motorway and followed the ring-road round the outskirts of Bradford. Like Sheffield, the city had grown along the valleys and up the hills but Bradford was built on wool not steel. My mobile began to bleat and I pulled in at a bus stop and fished it out of my bag.

'Sal Kilkenny.'

'Hello, it's St Paul's here, we've got Maddie and Tom waiting, no-one's come to collect them.'

I felt a wave of panic followed by a roll of anger. Where the hell was Ray? Had something happened to him? My mind span round seeking solutions. It would take me an hour or more to get back. Nana Tello wouldn't be able to do it, unless she could get a taxi and had the money to pay for it. I hadn't got Ray's college number on me and past experience had told me it was hopeless trying to contact him there. Besides Salford is miles from Withington, it'd take him ages to get to school.

'I'm ever so sorry, there's obviously been some mix up. I'm afraid I'm over in Yorkshire but I'll try and get somebody to come and get them now, I'll ring you back and let you know what's happening.'

I took the school's number then dialled home. Bloody Ray. No answer. Vicky? Vicky Dobson! Back from her tour of the festivals, she'd often babysat for Maddie and Tom before. I punched the number. Please be in, please.

''Lo?'

'Vicky, it's Sal. Look, it's a bit of an emergency. Ray's forgotten to pick the kids up from school. I'm in Bradford and I can't get there. Could you get them? I'd pay you

204

of course.'

'Yeah, sure.'

Oh, thank you, thank you, thank you.

'Shall I bring them back here?'

'Great. I'll come round as soon as I get back. I'll let the school know you're coming.'

So, I was extremely rattled by the time I rang the Shuttles doorbell. She answered.

'Mrs Shuttle?'

'Yes.'

'Sal Kilkenny, we spoke on the phone some time ago. I'm trying to trace Jennifer Pickering.'

Her expression changed; polite reserve hardening into appalled disbelief.

'I told you,' she said, 'I've nothing to say to you. How dare you come here...'

I cut her off. 'That's why I came. You're the only person who has refused to talk to me. That makes me curious.'

'Get out of here,' she said her voice quiet. At that point the door from the back garden swung open and a man appeared carrying a garden-vac. Mrs Shuttle froze, eyes like a rabbit in the road.

'Perhaps I should talk to your husband instead?' I smiled and made as if to turn.

'No,' she hissed. 'Come in.'

205

'I'll do the front now, Marjorie,' Mr Shuttle announced. 'Will you plug me in.' He came up with the cable, smiled expectantly at me.

'Hello,' I said brightly.

'Do come in,' Marjorie blurted out, taking the cable from him, 'this is Mrs Kenny, from Italian night class.'

'Ah, buongiorno,' he enunciated.

I nodded, grinning inanely and escaped into the house.

Marjorie Shuttle's efforts to hide who I was and what I was doing from her husband spoke volumes about her connection to the Pickerings. Whatever it was it was still secret. I waited until she'd plugged in the lead and called out to her husband and then went with her into their living room, at the back of the house. I sat down without being asked. Sod the niceties. I wasn't going to try and eke out dribs and drabs of information from Mrs Shuttle with carefully worded questions. She had something to hide and I was going to make her tell me about it. I'd start by making her think I already knew most of it.

'The business with the Pickerings. I'd like to hear your side of it.' As if I'd heard the other.

There was a fractional pause, she licked her lips. The drone of the vac reached us but was muffled by the distance. I looked towards the door, cocked my ear focusing on the sound then looked back to her, raised my eyebrows. Not very subtle, a nudge really, tell me or I ask him. She let out a long breath and stared at the carpet.

'I don't see what this has to do with anything,' she prevaricated. 'We haven't seen the Pickerings for over twenty years.'

'Mrs Shuttle, I've come a long way today, I'm tired. I realise this may not be easy for you but just tell me about it in your own words. Save us both some time.'

'This won't go any further?'

'Of course not.'

'If Gordon ever found out…'

'I'm not about to tell him but the longer I'm here the more risk there is that he'll suspect something – or interrupt us and I'd have to see you again then.'

She gave a big sigh and shifted her position, looked down at the rug and spoke. 'We were having an affair, Frank and I.'

Bloody 'ell!

I nodded, go on.

'He'd been very kind, very thoughtful. Helping in the garden and … well, Gordon, my husband, was away a lot, he was a rep, covered the whole of the North, right up to Scotland. I was lonely, I was very young,' she raised her eyes to me. 'But I hadn't thought of him in that way. Then one day, he found me crying, you see,' she studied the floor again, 'I was so unhappy and he comforted me. One thing led to another. It got out of control. I don't know how. It was very physical, very powerful. It was an awful shock for both of us. We promised it would never happen again, we tried to stop.'

She smiled grimly. 'It didn't make either of us happy, just the opposite, really. It was awful. We both knew it was wrong, that we might hurt other people. And Frank being so respected in the church and all that. But there was this attraction, a sexual thing. Like a compulsion, an addiction. We needed each other. We'd stop and try and get on with our lives but all I could think about was Frank. I never sought him out, though,' she added hastily. 'Days would go by, weeks sometimes and then he'd come back. Desperate. I couldn't refuse him, I wanted him. No-one had ever made me feel that way – physically, I mean. He said the same. I don't think he and Barbara had much of a marriage by then. Even when my mind was telling me it was wrong, my body was obsessed with him. And it would start all over again. The sex, then the guilt and the promises.'

'How long did this go on?'

'About a year. Then Jennifer found out, I don't know how,' she pre-empted me. 'Frank came round, he said Barbara knew, that Jennifer had found out.'

'And after that?'

'They cut me dead. I couldn't blame them. But it was terrible. I was so lonely and I couldn't talk to Gordon about any of it.'

'Who cut you dead?'

'Frank and Barbara?'

'And Jennifer?'

'She'd gone to university. I got very depressed, more depressed. I told Gordon we had to move, that I didn't like the house. It didn't matter to him, we could move further north, better for his job. We put it on the market, it took forever to find the right buyers,' she shuddered. She sat before me ashen-faced, hunched over, still plagued by the wretched emotions dredged up recalling that miserable affair. The whine outside stopped and suddenly the room was full of silence.

'Frank got ill,' I said.

'He wasn't the only one,' she retorted bitterly. She hid her face with her hands for a moment, then re-appeared. 'I'm sorry, that wasn't fair. Yes, it was his heart, they said. You can see why I didn't want to discuss any of this, it's nothing but bad memories for me.' She tilted her head to listen. Wondering where her husband was now. 'You better go,' she said nervously. 'Please.'

I thanked her for her time and prepared to leave.

'So Jennifer is missing?' she asked. Regaining the ground of polite conversation even as she willed me to be gone.

'Yes, she's been estranged from the family and now her brother Roger wants to find her.'

She nodded.

And how on earth, I thought, do I tell him about you?

I barely noticed the traffic on the drive back to Manchester, though now and again some prat would pull out in front of me at the last minute forcing me to brake or veer into the outside lane. Then I'd curse and huff and puff and wait for my skin to settle back round my body. But for the most of the journey my mind was buzzing with activity spinning scenes from the new facts I'd uncovered.

I was convinced that I was much nearer to solving one part of the riddle. I now had two possible explanations for Jennifer calling her father a hypocrite. Either because she had discovered her own illegitimate status and his reaction to her pregnancy was unjust, or because of his adultery. Thou shalt not covet thy neighbour's wife. She'd caught him breaking all the rules, betraying his family, breaking the commandment. That was when she'd rung Lisa.

How had Jennifer found out? Perhaps she'd called round one day, some errand for her mother, to borrow something or deliver a wrongly delivered letter. Only to find that her father was there, when he should be at the office or at church. The atmosphere at the Shuttles, the fleeting guilt of his greeting enough to alert the bright, young woman to the truth of the situation. But if that was how it happened Mrs Shuttle would have remembered, it'd be blazoned into her memory. OK. Same situation but Jennifer heard voices, her father's as well, or sounds of love-making as she reached the house. Peered through the letter-box to see. Heard her father's name called in passion, saw his briefcase in the hall, witnessed an embrace, there they were kissing, groping, screwing. The hypocrite.

Had Jennifer told her mother? I'd no reason to think of Jennifer as vindictive but families don't always bring out the best in people. Had she tackled her father? Or had she let it stew for a while, fermenting inside, pressure building until in the midst of an argument she'd blown her top and pointed the finger?

And how would her father have reacted? She was jeopardising everything: his marriage, his integrity, his status in the church and in business. I felt a lurch of anxiety and adrenalin prickled along my forearms. Had he tried to shut her up, stop her telling her mother? Had Jennifer flung the fact of her own pregnancy at him? You forgave her, so forgive me. Had she told him about Maxwell Jones? He's black but I'm not ashamed of it, I'm not prejudiced like you. Had she threatened to unmask him in the rush of her anger? Had he prevented her?

I tried to clear my mind, to think logically but the scene that I had conjured up kept creeping back in focus. It seemed preposterous but if he had killed Jennifer, if she had never left home, then her troll would be left in the window, she would miss Caroline's party, there'd be no goodbyes, no presents for her brother's birthdays, no admission to Keele, no word to anyone. Ever.

I had a whole heap of stuff to tell Roger. Not just a skeleton in the cupboard, more like a whole chorus-line of them, clattering out one after the other. Starting with; Jennifer is your half-sister, you've got different fathers, your mother had Jennifer out of wedlock, Jennifer was already three years old when your parents got married. Moving onto the news that your father had an affair with Mrs Shuttle, next door. Do you remember her? And Jennifer found out. On top of all that there's no record of Jennifer having a baby, no registered death, no marriage, no sign of her whatsoever. And to cap it all there's a very simple, ludicrous, nightmarish explanation for your sister's disappearance. It fits with all the facts but there isn't a shred of proof. All speculation. But before I breathe a word of that to you there's a couple of return visits I intend to make.

Chapter Sixteen

I came into Manchester in the height of the rush-hour but I was heading in the right direction. The log jam on the other side of the central reservation stretched nose to tail for miles.

I drove straight to the Dobson's to find Maddie and Tom having tea with the family. Eight of them in all crammed round the big table.

'Why did you forget?' Maddie scowled, 'It was horrible.'

'I didn't,' my anger at Ray re-kindled, 'Ray was supposed to collect you, I was working late.'

'Would you like some?' Jackie asked me. 'It's only pizza and salad.'

I hesitated.

'Go on,' said her husband Grant. 'I'll get another chair.'

I was soon ensconced, listening to the chatter of the Dobson girls as they re-counted incidents from school and updated Vicky on some of the scandals she'd missed during her trek round the festivals. I felt a tickle of worry about Ray. What if he'd been in an accident, unable to get to school through no fault of his own. Maybe I was judging him unfairly. I was keen to get home once we'd finished eating. As we were leaving I paid Vicky. 'I don't know what I'd have done if you hadn't been here, you're a lifesaver.'

She grinned.

The kids clambered into the hire car, suitably impressed and making all sorts of favourable noises.

'Mummy,' asked Maddie, 'can I have a nose stud?'

'Yeurgh, like a punk,' said Tom.

'No, you can't, not till you're grown up.'

'But that's ages.'

'Well, you'll just have to wait.'

'Please, can I?'

'No.'

'Why not?'

'Children don't have nose studs.'

'They have earrings.'

'Some do.'

'Well, if they can have them in their ears why can't I have one in my nose.'

I grappled for a reply. 'It's not allowed at school.' Cop out.

'You could write a note.'

'No.'

'I could take it out for school.'

I resorted to threats. 'It hurts, Maddie, they have to punch a hole in your nose with a special gun and it really stings.'

'Oh,' a small voice. Maddie is feeble when it comes to pain.

I felt mean. 'So it'd be best to wait until you're grown up. Meanwhile we could see if we could find some stick on studs you could wear at the weekend.'

'Yes, Mummy, yes.'

The house was dark. No sign of Ray. We'd been in a few minutes when he arrived back. I was washing the breakfast pots. He sauntered in. My relief was quickly replaced with mounting irritation. I felt my back stiffen. He glanced at the hob, peered in the fridge. Looking for his tea.

'You eaten? Nothing left?'

'We ate at the Dobsons.'

'Oh, you didn't say.'

'I didn't know.'

He heard the edge to my voice, shifted his stance, chin up a little, defiant.

'You were supposed to collect Maddie and Tom. I was half-way across the country and

I got a phone call from school. No-one had turned up.'

'Hang on a minute. Who says I was collecting them?'

'I asked you last night.'

'When?'

'Oh, for God's sake, I didn't make a note of the time. When I got in.'

He shook his head.

'Ray, I did. And you said yes.'

He carried on shaking his head, his curls bouncing as he did.

'I'm not making it up,' I insisted.

'Well, they're here now,' he snapped, 'it's not the end of the world, is it?'

'I was worried. It was pure chance that I could get hold of someone to go and pick them up. What if I hadn't been able to? What would have happened then?'

'The school would hardly turf them out on the street,' he retorted.

'It wasn't much fun for Maddie and Tom, either. I think you should apologise to them.' If not to me, I added silently.

'God! It's hardly a regular occurrence. And I don't think you asked me. What exactly did you say?' His dark eyes were hard with defiance.

I couldn't bear this wriggling round the

truth. Why couldn't he just accept the blame gracefully?

'I did,' I said.

'OK,' he shouted, 'even if you did and if I forgot – which I didn't – it's hardly a hanging offence is it?'

'If you hadn't been so wrapped up in Laura you might have paid a bit more attention to what was going on in the rest of the world.'

'Fuckin' 'ell.' Wide-eyed and outraged.

'I'm sorry, but I need to be able to rely on you, the kids need to. These days they hardly see you. When you are here, you...'

'I don't have to listen to this,' he stalked off.

'And I had to pay ten pounds for the babysitter.'

He stormed back in, slammed a ten pound note down on the table and left.

I sat down slowly, stunned at how heavy things had become. Was it me? If he'd only taken responsibility and apologised things would have been fine but all that casting aspersions on whether I'd asked him... How the hell would I be able to ask him about plans for the future with Laura, now? Oh no! I was meeting Diane later. We'd arranged to have a drink at one of the new café bars in Didsbury. Diane had talked me into it. We ought to try somewhere new, she'd said, I had my reservations. But had Ray remembered? For a stupid moment I considered getting Vicky Dobson to babysit to avoid asking Ray but that would cost money. It was pathetic, too. I would get the kids ready for bed, have a bath myself and then tackle him.

Maddie and Tom were in their playroom. Tom was smashing farm animals into each other and yelling various threats at them, Maddie was absorbed in a Polly Pocket toy. All our attempts to raise them free from gender stereotypes had come to this. The room was strewn with books, games, dressing-up clothes, pens and play-food. It looked like someone had trashed the place.

'Time to clear up.'

Tom groaned, Maddie ignored me.

'Maddie, come on, I'll help and it'll soon be done.'

She slammed Polly's palace down and flung back her head with a sigh.

'Let's see how quickly we can do it? I'll count.' The old trick worked with Tom who began to hurl toys into the plastic boxes along the wall but Maddie was having none of it. She moved in slow-motion. I felt a flash of irritation but directed it into lugging armfuls of clothes into the dressing-up hamper. I'd had enough rows for one day. Still, I couldn't resist a snippy comment when we were done. 'We'd have done it even quicker if Maddie had helped. If you're that tired, Maddie, you'd better have an early night.'

'Aw, Mum.'

'Ha-ha,' said Tom.

'Shut-up,' she flounced out.

'Bath-time now,' I called after her.

They always come out of the bath happier than when they go in. That's the main reason for doing it. After all they don't get a chance to get that dirty at school and they hadn't been playing out. I got them settled and allowed them to listen to one short tape, citing Maddie's tiredness again. She grinned at me.

My turn. Once in the bath, with added bath salts, I slid down until only my head was out of the water. I closed my eyes and let my thoughts drift. I put a face cloth over my eyes and floated for a while. The tension in my muscles from the driving and the aggro began to loosen. When my wrinkles had wrinkles and the water was cooling I got out. Like the children I emerged feeling better; oh, a host of worries still hovered over work and the argy-bargy with Ray but I didn't feel so battered by them.

I got ready. Ray was on the phone. As I came downstairs he went quiet. Talking about me? Telling Laura about my unjust accusations? Would she remember that I'd asked him? Would she say so? I didn't know her well enough to judge. In the kitchen Digger raised his head, spotted me and lowered it again. Ray showed no sign of getting off the phone so I wrote a note in felt tip on the back of a letter from school advising us of another head-lice outbreak.

Am going out now. I wondered whether to add *Remember?* But decided *OK?* would be more tactful. I went into the hall and held the message up in front of him. He put his hand over the mouthpiece, scanned the paper and nodded curtly. I pinned the note back on the board in the kitchen to remind me to check the kids' hair the next day.

I put on my cycling helmet and my jacket and got my bike out of the shed at the end of drive. I knew I'd be having a couple of drinks and I didn't want to drink and drive. Drinking and cycling I felt OK with; I didn't regard my bike in the same league as a car when it came to capacity to inflict damage.

I knew it was technically possible to be drunk in charge of bicycle but I never got to that stage. My front light seemed a bit dim, I couldn't believe how fast they devoured batteries and broke bulbs. Super built-in obsolescence like torches, irons and toasters, but tons quicker.

It's only a mile or so to Didsbury, more upmarket than Withington with some very expensive properties. The last couple of years had seen lots of development, new supermarkets, a plethora of restaurants and café bars and of course lots of new houses crammed into the old Waterfords Dairy site to bring in some customers for all the leisure outlets.

It took me longer to get all my clobber on and then off and lock up the bike and remove the lights than it did to make the journey.

The bar Diane had chosen was already heaving. One look at it and I wanted to leave but she'd already bought me a drink and managed to find a table in a corner by the toilets. Most of the clientele preferred to stand, presumably to show off their designer gear and to spot the talent. Most of them were fresh-faced and full of life, I don't know how many of them were old enough to drink legally.

'I thought it'd only be like this at weekends,' Diane apologised. We had to lean close to each other to talk, the noise was tremendous.

'So, how was it?'

She smiled but it was hard for me to read it. At least she wasn't crying. Which is what I remember her doing a lot of the last time Ben had been in the picture.

'Good,' she nodded. 'I'd forgotten how much he made me laugh. We had a wonderful Thai meal the first night and the next day I did some galleries. Oh, and I met this buyer, very interested in my work. I promised I'd send her some slides. Ben had a meeting in the morning but we met for lunch and then he took me shopping.'

I studied her. Had some alien invaded Diane's body (apart from Ben)? Since when did anybody 'take' Diane shopping? She sounded like a Stepford wife. 'He wanted to treat me,' she went on, 'it was like one of those 40's films, you know, with Cary Grant waiting for the dame in the posh ladies dress emporium.'

I envisaged the scene. All peach drapes and soft carpets and huge mirrors. Diane, surrounded by starlet sylphs in silk camisoles. Diane with her inky fingers, her wild hair-styles, her Doc Martens and her size 20 frame.

'What did you get?'

'These.' She turned her ankle to show me an electric blue Doc Marten. Phew.

'And a gorgeous chenille top and a full length dress, indigo crushed velvet.'

'Go well with the Docs.'

She grinned and leant closer, 'And some very sexy underwear.' She rolled her eyes.

'So you slept with him,' I said bluntly.

'Yes. And it was great.'

'And now?'

'I don't know,' she said. 'He's getting married. We haven't made any plans.' She seemed blase about it but I felt uncomfortable.

'So it was just a final fling?'

'It wasn't just anything,' her eyes flashed. 'Stop being so bloody uptight. We met, we talked, there was a lot of unfinished business. It was good to have a chance to talk it over. And, yes, we went to bed together. He's not married yet, you know.'

'Diane, how would you feel if you were getting married to someone and they went off in search of an ex-lover for a last screw?'

She looked at me steadily. 'She'll never

know. We're all grown up, Sal.'

Doesn't mean you always act like it, though. 'Will you see him again?'

She shrugged.

'And that's OK?'

Even with the racket all around us, I could hear her silence; loud like an alarm. She wanted him, she'd lost him but now she would settle for this, the odd visit every year or so. I couldn't bear it. She'd be like the mistresses featured in documentaries; never having the important times, never the whole night, the holiday, always a secret, always waiting. I wanted her to be strong and independent, like she usually was, not to compromise one iota. I thought of Mrs Shuttle and her miserable affair with Frank Pickering. Secrecy. Didn't seem to bring much happiness.

I swerved the conversation away, told her about my bust-up with Ray. We agreed that all I could do was ask him directly for a time to talk, about the house, about the future.

We had finished our drinks. I struggled to the bar, waited impatiently to be served and did a double-take at the cost.

I put the drinks down. 'And I had my car nicked.'

'Oh, no. From home?'

'No, this place in Hulme, where I'm working. I was there on Monday night. There was lots of trouble and we had to call the police but the guy that came was a right waste of space, worse really. You could tell he sympathised with the racists and he didn't give a shit for the family being hounded.' I told her about the events that night. 'Then, I'm finally ready to go home and my car's gone. I haven't heard anything yet.'

'So do you reckon they'll be able to kick them out now?'

'I hope so. I've sent the tape in so I'll find out what they think tomorrow. I mean, even if there's a wait while they prepare the court case, they need to get the victims out of there or give them protection or something. It's so savage. I was watching these lads and thinking where does all that hate come from? How do you change people like that?'

'I don't think you can,' she took a drink. 'What about that other thing, the girl who disappeared in the 70's?'

'Oh, don't ask,' I groaned.

'That bad?'

I nodded. 'It's like this Pandora's box of secrets. I went to the Records Office yesterday and it turns out the girl was illegitimate

226

and yet she's being brought up in this really strict household where they are all leading highly moral lives, setting an example for the flock, 'cos Daddy's a preacher. Only it turns out he's having a fling with the next door neighbour.'

'And she was pregnant herself wasn't she, the girl?' asked Diane.

'Yes.'

'Did she know her mother had been in the same position?'

'I don't think so. She'd have said something to her mates, don't you reckon? None of them mentioned it.' I took a drink. 'And everyone thought she'd gone to university and then dropped out but it turns out she never made it.'

'Sounds like a real mess.'

'It is and what worries me most...'

'Diane?' There was a man bending over our table. No-one I knew but Diane seemed pleased to see him.

'Hiya, Stuart. How ya doing?' Maybe one of her lonely-hearts dates. She'd been on plenty. That's how she'd met Desmond. What would she tell him about her reunion with Ben? Anything?

Stuart glanced my way a few times. He was attractive but I observed him dispassionately. I'd got out of the habit of clocking the talent, or of acting on it. Pretty men were like beautiful gardens; something I noted as I walked on by.

Well, they were usually.

'This is Sal,' Diane said, 'Stuart Bowker.'

He gave me a smile and asked me a question, looking intently at me as though I was the most interesting thing in the universe. I can't remember what it was or how I replied, I was too mortified trying to control the blush that was colour-washing my whole body. So humiliating.

He had good teeth, even, with a slight gap in the middle, a large mouth. I couldn't tell whether his eyes were blue or brown, a mix perhaps. His hair was grey, cut extremely short. He laughed at something I said. Or maybe he was laughing at me. At last he turned back to Diane. I tried to compose myself.

'Catch you later,' he said.

I felt sick. As he moved away the volume of noise from the punters at the bar seemed to mushroom. Another crowd came in, the girls wore what passed for underwear in my day and the boys looked ready for the ski slopes, all thick fleeces and puffer jackets. They clustered by our table. We were hemmed in.

'So, what do you think?' Diane asked.

'I prefer our usual. It's too loud and it's hardly relaxing. I'm ready for off.'

She narrowed her eyes at me.

'What?'

'Stuart. What do you think of Stuart.'

So that was it. She'd lured me here to weigh up a new conquest of hers – or someone she'd got her eye on.

'Don't you think you've got enough on your plate?' I pulled my jacket on.

'Not me. You.'

It was my turn to glare. 'Diane! What do you think you were...' raising my voice above the racket made me cough as the smoke caught in my throat.

I fought my way out and she followed. We went round to the carpark where our bikes were.

'What did you tell him?' I was all outrage.

'Nothing, give me some credit. But if you're interested I can always invite him to something.'

'I don't need a matchmaker. I'm not looking for a match. I'm perfectly happy as I am. Just because you want...'

'Go on,' she said dangerously.

'I'm not you,' I pointed out. 'You want a

relationship, you've done the ads, you've met Desmond. That's great but don't assume I want the same.'

'You don't want a relationship? Not ever?'

'I didn't say that.'

'They don't fall from the skies you know, you have to go looking. You fancied him, didn't you?'

'I don't know,' I muttered, trying to get my key in the bike lock.

'He's lovely man,' she said.

'So how come he's available then?'

'Divorced.'

'Oh,' I groaned.

'And over it,' she insisted. 'Good relationship with his ex. They share the kids, all very amicable.'

He had children.

I got the lock sorted out and put my helmet on.

'Think about it,' she said.

He might not fancy me, though.

'Anyway, if he's such a lovely man, what's he doing in a place like this? It wasn't just coincidence. Did you tell him to come?' I got all agitated again.

She laughed. 'No. There was a pretty good chance he'd be here, anyway. He's the boss. This is his place.'

Later I was still a bit peeved that Diane had engineered the meeting without asking me about it first but there was also a positive side to it. My mind got side-tracked into weaving fantasies about Stuart Bowker and that left me no room to dwell on the fate of Jennifer Pickering, my row with Ray or the plight of the Ibrahim family.

Bedtime was more fun than usual.

Chapter Seventeen

Next morning there was a message from Roger on the ansaphone at the office. He was eager to know what I'd found out. I wasn't ready to give him a full report yet. I wanted to talk again to Mrs Clerkenwell. I needed to try and fix as much as I could about the last known movements of Jennifer and something was niggling at me. I was sure there was some significance behind the incident when Jennifer had turned and run from Frances's. Once I had checked that out I would tackle Mrs Pickering and see if she had anything to say that would disprove my theory. Then I'd go to Roger.

In the meantime the least I could do was give him the bald facts about my research. No baby, no marriage, no death and tell him I was making a few final enquiries to verify everything before I gave him my complete report.

When he answered the phone I proceeded to flatten the hope in his voice.

'Isn't there anything else you can try?'

'No. I don't think so. I'm sorry,' I concluded. 'Can we meet next Monday perhaps, lunchtime, say twelve-thirty? That'll give me time to write up all the details for you.'

'So it's just a dead-end?' he asked.

I closed my eyes at the irony. 'It looks that way.'

Mandy Bellows was off sick. When I asked if anyone was covering her work-load I got laughed at. 'She should be in next week though.' And until she was, nothing was going to move forward for the Ibrahims.

Mr Poole was dismayed when I called him. 'I'm going to have a word with the councillor about this. One person's off and the whole thing grinds to a standstill.'

'Hopefully, she'll be in on Monday and I'll ring her first thing, tell her to make it a priority. I've still got the camera so if anything happens meanwhile let me know.'

'What's this I hear about your car?'

'It went on Monday, just as I was ready for home and there was no sign of it.'

'How did you get back?'

'I got a taxi.'

'You should have woken me, you could have rung from here.'

'No. I had my mobile. Anyway, how did you hear about it?'

'The Brennans,' he said, 'making cracks about it. Took me a while to cotton on.'

'They probably took it but I can't prove anything.'

'Have they found it yet? They could finger-print it.'

'No. No word. Besides I'd rather see them lose the tenancies or get bound over to keep the peace than done for nicking my car. Least I'm insured.'

My last call was to Mrs Clerkenwell. I arranged an appointment with her that afternoon.

The hire car was due back but I made use of it to get some shopping from the green-grocers and the small supermarket in Withington. I stocked up on some of the basics and bulky items as I didn't know how long I'd be without a car and they were awkward to carry on the bike. I left the lot at home and took the car in. I walked back to the office enjoying the colours of the leaves which were brilliant in the sunshine. Frost still edged the foliage in shady corners and covered puddles with sheets of ice.

I had a cup of coffee and then worked solidly on my notes from the Records Office and my summary of the case so far. When I document a job I usually include a section which no-one ever sees where I jot down all the wild, implausible, outrageous notions that I have as to what may have happened. Now and then I hit on something and it's a useful way for me to see things from another angle. It's also a good way of getting any pet theories out of my system and of exposing them to the light. Once they are written down I find I can discount some of them. But I was reluctant to go through this process with Jennifer Pickering. There was some superstitious side of me that feared that if I committed my imaginings to paper they might come true. And I wanted to be wrong this time.

I collected my bike from home and cycled up to the baths to do my regular twenty lengths. One of the other swimmers reminded me of Stuart Bowker and I had a fierce impulse to run and hide. A second look told me it wasn't him. I felt a flutter of embarrassment. I swam away from it. Did I want a relationship? My gut reaction was no. It all seemed too complicated, too much trouble. How could I start something like that without disrupting my life? How would Maddie take it? Did I want to meet Stuart again. Yes. Yes, I did. And the thought brought bubbles to my insides and made me kick my legs harder and spread my arms wider and swim that bit faster.

Mrs Clerkenwell put the dogs out before she let me in. She'd obviously been working; her hair was covered by a scarf and she wore a large calico smock which she removed to reveal the same dark trousers and woolly jumper as on my first visit.

'Any news?' She asked me once we had sat down.

'No, I'm afraid not. But I wanted to ask you about a couple of things, to try and make sense of what other people have told me. I can't go into details, confidentiality, you see. And the questions may seem a bit strange.'

'I'm intrigued. Fire away.'

I thought back to Frances's account of her last time with Jennifer. That moment when

Jennifer had become so distressed. 'OK. From your garden you can see a fair bit of the house behind and vice-versa.'

She bobbed up to refresh her memory. 'Yes.'

'If you were out in the garden you'd have a clear view of the upstairs but not of the ground floor, because of the wall?'

'That's right. If you wanted to see into their garden or their kitchen or whatever you'd have to be upstairs here.'

'Or on the wall.'

'Erm … yes.' She smiled enjoying the game we were playing.

'Now, suppose someone was on the wall at the bottom of the Pickerings' garden. They'd have a good view across here but they wouldn't see much of the Pickerings' or of the house on the other side.'

'The Kennedys',' she said.

'Yes, with the trees along the bottom and the big hedge down the side.'

'Hedge!' she snorted. 'They're a liability, those things, grow like Triffids. I said to Mr Kennedy when they planted them that they'd be up and down ladders trimming them every five minutes.'

My neck prickled. 'They weren't there when the Shuttles had the house?'

'Oh, no. They just had an ordinary fence and the sycamores at the end so they weren't overlooked from the back anyway, not like I am.'

I walked over to the French windows and looked out.

She carried on talking. 'Those things must be eight foot high. You could have seen over before.'

Bingo! I pictured Jennifer astride the wall, her father and Mrs Shuttle seen from her vantage point. 'But the shed would have blocked the view.'

'Well, that wasn't always there either. Frank put that up.'

I looked at her. 'When?' My mouth was dry.

She screwed up her face. 'Let's see. It must have been before he got ill, he did it all himself. Yes, it was. I remember they thought that had brought on the angina, too much for him. So that must have been...' she calculated.

I knew what was coming.

'...in the autumn, 1976. The ground was like concrete.'

The blood in my veins stopped moving.

'He'd had a bed there, perennials, a lovely show but that heat killed them. I think he gave up. Decided to call it quits. It's a merciless spot there, there's never any shade. He might have got away with roses,' she shrugged, returned from her reverie. 'That any help?'

'Yes.' Now I could explain how Jennifer, atop the dividing wall, had discovered her father's adultery. What she glimpsed sent her scrambling in the other direction, appalled and inarticulate. What she saw had triggered the confrontation that followed.

And now I knew where Jennifer was. I tried to swallow, my throat was tight and a twist of panic played in my stomach.

'I know it's a long time ago,' I said, 'but can you remember any disturbances from next door, early autumn 1976, just before Jennifer left home? Any rows, raised voices, that sort of thing?'

'No. I've not got that sort of recall. I know I'm good on names but dates, when things happen...' she shook her head.

'You said before that you heard raised voices sometimes?'

'Yes, but I couldn't say when, exactly. And it wasn't that often. The walls here are quite thick, and I was out and about a lot with the business. I mean, they did have words now and then, I'd hear it if I was in the garden

238

and they'd left the window open but there's no particular time I recall.'

'And you would hear Mr Pickering shouting or Jennifer?'

'Yes. He had a temper and Jennifer, well at that age they are prone to flare up, aren't they?'

'Thanks,' I finished the interview.

'I'll be awake all night wondering what's behind these questions,' her eyes twinkled.

Me too. I tried to act normally while I bade farewell to Mrs Clerkenwell and not to let my eyes ricochet wildly about like my thoughts were.

My hands were trembling as I unlocked my bike. I had an overwhelming urge to run away, as though I was the guilty one. Knowing what I did made me feel dirty. What was I going to do about it? The police? They'd show me the door straightaway, surely. Everything I had was circumstantial. There were no eye-witnesses to any wrong doing. There was no shred of evidence that anything untoward had befallen Jennifer Pickering – I didn't think an abandoned troll would count for much. She was missing, that's all. A statistic.

I was sure though, gut sure, that Jennifer had never left home. Her body lay in the garden, under the shed that her father had built around her, a mausoleum for a murder. Soon his breaking heart and guilty conscience had made him sick and driven him to despair and death. She had lain there and festered, a macabre secret that would never have been uncovered had Roger not longed to see his sister again.

What would I tell him? I reeled away from the prospect and the bike lurched unsteadily. Before I told anything to a soul I had to talk to Mrs Pickering again and confront her with the lies she had told. She must have known, she must have done. It was she who said Jennifer had gone to Keele and later dropped out. She must have helped him hide the body, hide the truth from Roger. No wonder the garden had gone to rack and ruin. Could either of them have stepped outside without recalling what was buried there? Had any of them ever used the shed? Had Roger played in it as a den? I had a wave of revulsion. How could she sleep at night?

My concentration was shot when I got home. I went to make a cup of tea but forgot to switch the kettle on; it helps the water to boil if you include electricity in the equation. When I got that sorted I found myself making two cups one after the other.

I tried to piece together the correct sequence of events. Jennifer had seen her father and Mrs Shuttle from the wall. She'd run off. Later she had spoken to Lisa and called her father a hypocrite. Had she told her mother? Or maybe she had threatened her father with her knowledge first or tried to make a trade-off; I'll keep quiet if you support me and my baby; I'm pregnant you see. There was no deal made. Jennifer was silenced. Jennifer disappeared.

I checked the number and dialled the Bradford number.

'Hello, can I speak to Mrs Shuttle please? It's Mrs Kenny from Italian.'

She came on the line her voice taut with suspicion. 'What is it?'

'Just one question, when Frank Pickering told you it was over, that Jennifer had found out, did he say whether Jennifer had told Barbara or whether he had to?'

'I don't know.'

'It's important.'

'I think,' she lowered her voice, 'I think he just said that Barbara knew and when I asked him how, he said Jennifer had found out.'

'But not that Jennifer had told her?'

'It's a long time ago.'

'So after he broke it off how did you feel when you next saw Jennifer?'

'I didn't see her again, she'd gone off to university.'

Thank you.

I drank my tea too quickly, scalding my throat. I was late for school. I couldn't find my keys anywhere. I checked my pockets, the table, the shelf, the worktops. They'd gone. In the end I decided I would have to leave the door on the latch, I set the snib, went out and pulled it to behind me. My keys were there, dangling from the lock.

Ray mistook my preoccupation with work for an extended sulk. He's the sulky one usually, I'm more apt to lay the cards on the table or just lose my temper. He matched my silence with his own but I barely registered until Tom piped up. 'Why's everybody all grumpy?'

'I'm not,' Maddie said.

'Just tired,' Ray lied.

'I'm thinking about work,' I said, 'and that's making me grumpy.'

'Think about something happy, then,'

Maddie suggested.

'I'll try.'

'Think about Christmas presents.'

'And sweets.'

I cleared the table as the two of them invented outrageous wish lists based on all the television adverts they'd been watching.

Ray called Digger and they went off for walkies.

I had other creatures to attend to. 'Maddie, Tom, we need to check your hair.'

They groaned in unison.

It was a regular palaver. I smothered their hair with conditioner then combed it through several times with a nit comb.

Time was we'd had to use a range of chemical treatments that filled the room with fumes and made our eyes water, but Manchester lice had become immune and the authorities feared we were in danger of poisoning our children; like sheep that were dipped too often they might end up twitching and collapsing, nerves and immune systems shot at, hence the conditioner and comb.

I found nothing on Tom.

'Don't tell me, Mummy,' Maddie instructed me as she bent over the basin so I kept it to myself, tapped the two adult-sized beasties into the sink and rinsed them away. I then applied herbal shampoo designed to deter lice to each scalp and put them in the bath for quarter of an hour while the lotion did its stuff. My head itched. I would do myself later.

While Ray was out I rehearsed what I would say when he got back. By the time I'd washed up, tidied the kitchen and swept the floor I was word perfect.

I heard the door open then Digger ambled into the kitchen followed by Ray. I didn't even give him time to take his jacket off.

'I think we should have a talk, Ray. Can we fix a time?'

He sighed theatrically. 'If this is all about yesterday...' he began.

'It's not just that, there are other things and I'd rather we discussed them when we've got time to do it properly. One evening perhaps?'

'I can't do this weekend,' he said quickly.

'Next week sometime, Monday, Tuesday?'

'Tuesday.'

'After they're in bed.'

He nodded and wandered out. I let go of the tea-towel that I'd been gripping so firmly and rubbed at the cramp in my hand.

Chapter Eighteen

I was restless that evening. I wanted, more than anything, to pamper myself, to relax. I went through the motions; opened a bottle of red wine, got my book and a snack ready, tidied my room, had scented candles in my bath. It was all very pleasant but my mind was locked on Jennifer Pickering. I even tried day-dreaming about Stuart Bowker but he kept sliding away to be replaced by other visions: Jennifer shouting at her father, Frank feverishly building the shed, Barbara clearing out her daughter's room. There was a constant churning in my guts.

Finally I slept. In my dream I was yelling at Mrs Pickering who was forcing soil into my mouth. Ray stood beside her watching. Then he began to call my name.

'Sal, Sal.'

I woke with a muggy headache and a furry mouth. Ray stood in my doorway. I felt an irrational surge of anger at how he had betrayed me in the dream.

'Phone for you.'

I reached the phone expecting Diane, who, not having children, doesn't know the meaning of an early night.

'Sal, it's Mr Poole, there's trouble again – they're back outside the house, calling names and that, a big gang of them.'

'Right, I'll be there as soon as I can.'

I stumbled around getting my bag with the video camera, disguise, phone, keys. I washed two paracetamols down with a glass of water. I knew I shouldn't mix them with alcohol but if my headache got much worse I'd barely be able to function.

'Becoming a bit of a habit,' Ray said when I reached the kitchen.

'Yes, I'll be glad when this job's over.' And the other one, I thought. I'd solved the mystery of Jennifer's disappearance but I'd yet to disclose it to anyone and I wasn't looking forward to the response I'd get. Truth or not I felt like a pariah.

I rang for a cab. I watched out of the window for it to arrive. The wind had got up and was blowing hard at the trees. Carrier bags went careering down the street. Dark clouds were moving swiftly against a darker sky and across a creamy, full moon.

I climbed into the taxi and V. Chowdury greeted me.

'I got the call,' he said, 'recognised the address. You on a job then?'

I felt a rush of confusion. I didn't want to endanger the guy by asking him to drive me to the Close where the bully boys were out in force but would it be right to refuse to ride with him because of his race? How could I explain?

'This might not be a very good idea.'

'What?'

'I'm going back to Canterbury Close, in Hulme, where you picked me up before.'

'Yeah.'

'The reason I'm going is there's some racists, kicking up trouble, they're harassing a family on the Close and I'm filming it for evidence. They could just as easily turn on you.'

'I can look after myself,' he said coolly.

'Maybe,' I said, 'but I don't want to put anyone else at risk. Isn't there someone else, another driver who could take me?'

I meant a white driver but couldn't quite bring myself to state it.

'No.'

'I could ring another firm.' I was thinking aloud.

'Look, I'll drop you nearby,' he said. 'That do you?'

There wasn't time to quibble and I thought he'd probably be alright doing that. The trouble would be down the Close and we could stop up on the main road.

'Are you sure?'

'I'm not the one who's bothered. I told you; I can look after myself.'

'OK, thanks.'

He roared off and got us there in just over seven minutes. He pulled up a few yards from the junction. 'They've blocked it off,' he said.

'Oh, God.'

A row of wheelie bins, an old mattress, scrap metal, the shell of a car (not mine), and the remains of a fridge freezer were strewn across the road.

I opened the door to see more clearly. Three boys, maybe nine or ten years old, peered from behind the bins. 'Fuck off,' one of them shouted.

I got out and went closer, 'What's going on?'

'Mind your own fuckin' business.'

'I need to get through.'

'What for?'

'See my uncle.'

'Who's he then?'

'Mr Poole.'

'He's a grass he is, old farty arse.'

I was sure they'd resist any attempt I made to clear the junk away. I walked back towards the taxi; maybe we could drive round and find the alleyway that led into the bottom of the Close.

A police siren grew closer and soon the flashing lights appeared round the bend. The car slewed to a halt by the barricade. I got my bag out of the taxi and retraced my steps. The taxi-driver got out and followed me.

'Come on, lads,' it was PC Doyle, the bigot. 'Clear this lot out of the way.' He made it sound like a weary request.

'We never done it,' one of the lads piped up.

'Shift it,' he barked.

The kids ran off, one of them hurled a load of abuse as he went.

The copper glanced at me and the cabbie.

'You best be off,' he said.

'I need to get through,' I said.

'You don't live round here,' he challenged.

'My uncle, Mr Poole, I'm staying there.'

He looked at me, eyes heavy with mistrust. Then he flicked his glance to the taxi-driver.

'Well, you can be on your way, Abdul,' he said. He began to pull one of the wheelie bins aside.

'The name's Johnny,' said the cabbie. I could hear the effort of control in his voice.

'I don't care if it's Mahatma bleeding Ghandi,' he yanked another bin to the kerb, 'get on your flying carpet and piss off.' He stopped to pull at a length of rusted metal and hurled it across to the pavement. He grimaced, his hands were filthy from the rust.

'What's your problem?' Johnny demanded.

'Hang on a minute,' I protested to Doyle, 'you can't...'

He wheeled round, confronting Johnny. 'You are getting in my way and if you don't move it, now, I'm charging you with obstruction, got that?' He stood, hands on hip, a grin of irritation on his face.

'This is crazy,' I began.

'You too, girlie,' he snapped. Then turning back to Johnny, 'Move it, paki, now.'

Johnny stared back, face set, eyes blazing.

'Right,' the policeman lunged, span him round and rammed his right arm up his back hard.

'Let him go,' I shouted.

'Get in the car,' yelled Doyle, pushing Johnny towards the white saloon. 'I'm arresting you on charges of obstruction and assaulting a police officer. You do not have to say anything but should you fail to mention,' he rattled off the long caution without pausing for breath as I ran after them. At the car Johnny stiffened. Doyle threw open the door. 'Get in the car, get in the car,' he roared, 'get in the fucking car.'

'Get off my arm,' Johnny shouted back.

'Get in the fucking car, now.'

He bundled Johnny in. There were wolf whistles and cheers from the smaller kids, I couldn't see them but they were watching the whole shebang.

'What are you messing about with him for?' I demanded of Doyle. 'He's done nothing. There's that lot down there to worry about. There's a mother and three kids in that house, it's them you should be thinking about.'

What was he planning to do with Johnny? Take him back to the police station, stopping on the way to 'teach him a lesson', hitting him where the bruises wouldn't show? Or claiming that any marks were down to Johnny's own violence when Doyle tried to arrest him? Anything could happen.

What if Doyle let the Brennans get at Johnny? I felt sick to my stomach. I'd watch him like a hawk. And I could always get the camera out if Doyle tried anything stupid. He wouldn't like his 'community policing approach' recorded on film, I was sure of that.

Doyle stalked off and began dragging things out of the way.

I bent down and spoke through the window so Johnny could hear me. 'I'm sorry. Look, we'll sort it out, we'll sort something out. Are you OK?'

He glared at me. I suppose it was a daft question.

As soon as I could, I would register an official complaint against PC Doyle but before then I had to get through and do my job. The quickest way to do that was to help clear the road. I went over to the other side of the road from Doyle and began shifting stuff to the roadside; a greasy bike frame, a heavy car door, its metal squealing as I scraped it along the tarmac. We'd soon cleared the way.

PC Doyle returned to his car and drove through. I picked up my bag and followed them down the Close. As soon as we had passed I heard the noise of the junk as the kids returned to rebuild their barricade.

There was an ugly atmosphere on the street. The police car had stopped directly outside the Ibrahims and a crowd were milling round it. I picked out the familiar faces of the trouble-makers I knew from among the many that I'd not seen before. Where had they all come from? They were singing an obscene song and clapping in time. They kept it up as PC Doyle got out of his car. Mr Poole stood in his front garden. I went over to greet him.

'You called the police?' I asked quietly.

'Yes, straight after I rang you. They were pouring stuff on the door, chanting like mad things.'

'Come along now,' Doyle shouted, 'let's break it up.'

'Who's that in yer car?' someone yelled.

'You'll have to fumigate it after he gets out, stink like fuck won't it?'

'What's he done then, eh?'

'Vindaloo, vindaloo, vindaloo, vindaloo,' they chanted.

Doyle pulled a megaphone from the boot of his car and tried again. 'Come on now, lads. You've had your fun.'

'Fun,' I muttered to Mr Poole.

'Why should we go home? Why can't they go home? This is our country.' It was Mr Whittaker speaking, his thin face etched with lines and rigid with hatred. 'We never asked them to come here. Fuckin' wogs. They get an house and they put their kids in our schools and they take our jobs.' The crowd mumbled agreement. 'Send them back. Dirty niggers. We don't want them round here.' A ragged, angry cheer erupted. I could see Johnny, tense and still in the car. I felt a wobble of guilt. I should have refused to let him drive me.

The crowd began to move about, like some restless beast, surging down to the bottom of the Close and back again. Circling up and down the road in a sinister parade. There must have been about fifty people there, mostly men and boys. Two or three of them wove mountain bikes on and off the pavements. There were a huddle of people down at the alleyway between the Whittaker and Brennan houses.

'I ought to get the camera going,' I said to Mr Poole. As if on cue a section of the mob surged forward towards the Ibrahims' and a volley of stones, bricks and bottles smashed against the house. The upstairs window cracked across.

Doyle spoke into his radio, presumably he'd got the sense to call for back-up. His eyes ranged across the crowd. No jokes with the lads now. He finished the call and lowered his radio. There was a new expression on his face, he swallowed, adjusted his hat. PC Doyle was frightened.

The door of the house adjacent to the Ibrahims' opened and a young couple came out. She hugged a child, who was sucking a dummy, to one hip and he had a dog on a lead.

'Bloody sick of this,' she shouted to the policeman, her face haggard in the streetlight. 'Why don't you sort them fuckers out?'

'Come on, leave it,' her husband grabbed her by the elbow.

'Gerroff,' she screeched.

The child began to wail.

'You're no bloody use you lot, you let them roam around like animals...'

Some of the crowd had clocked that she was talking about them and began to yell abuse back at her.

'Leave it, will ya,' the man yelled again and pulled her away. They hurried off up the Close. I looked down the road. Here and there I could see people peering from upstairs windows or stood on doorsteps. Watching, keeping a distance.

I felt uneasy about going into Mr Poole's to set up the camera and losing sight of Johnny in the police car. Surely they wouldn't try and hurt him while he was in the car. But if the violence increased, and the mob got a taste of its power, one copper wasn't going to prevent them doing whatever they wanted. I hesitated.

People continued to promenade up and down. They were using the houses at the bottom as a base, going down and coming back with cans and bottles. Free drinks for the occasion? I heard a siren again, in the distance but growing louder. The noise excited the crowd who began to clap and sing. There was a palpable sense of violence in the atmosphere. It was raising the hairs on my arms, tightening my spine, souring my mouth, heightening my senses. The siren stopped. There was no sign of the police. My heart sank. Had they gone? Was it another call they were going to?

Doyle looked uneasy, standing woodenly beside his car, radio in hand still. Eyes shifting about. He licked at his lips repeatedly. Then he opened the door and got into his car. Yells greeted his retreat and someone threw a drinks can which bounced off the windscreen. Were they going to storm the car? What about Johnny?

At last the strobe of blue light reached us heralding the arrival of the back-up. But it wasn't a van full of riot police or dogs, just another patrol car. Carl Benson and his partner pulled up behind Doyle's car and got out. The crowd applauded and someone set them off humming a rendition of the theme tune to 'The Bill'.

Doyle climbed out and Carl spoke to him, gesturing to show that the road was still blocked.

There was a sudden flurry of movement from the mob and another hail of missiles flew at the house. A bottle smashed against the front door, a bottle with a burning rag in it, and exploded in sheets of flame with a ferocity that made everyone rear back. A petrol bomb.

Chapter Nineteen

'Call the fire brigade,' Carl yelled and Doyle spoke into his radio.

I turned to Mr Poole, he had a look of despair on his face.

'Oh, God,' I said.

'I'll get some water,' he said.

More missiles followed, they were coming in waves. I pushed my way through to reach the police, I was jostled on the way and someone tried to trip me up. It was uncanny how they all seemed to know I wasn't part of the mob.

'The engines won't be able to get through,' I shouted to the police, 'they keep blocking the road up.'

Doyle scowled at me but Carl Benson's partner nodded and got back into their car. He reversed it up the Close.

Another bottle smashed against the front of the house, below the boarded up window and burst into flames. The paint on the door was bubbling and the small frosted glass panel near the top exploded with the heat.

The glass landed with a tinkling sound. The stench of petrol filled the air.

The fire lit up the faces of the crowd. People were jostling each other, calling and cheering, getting drunk on the spectacle. My stomach twisted but I ignored the fear and concentrated on the practical. Water.

I pushed my way back and met Mr Poole in his hallway. He had a large, black bucket of water. I left my bag there and took it from him, it weighed a ton. I staggered into the road with it, ignoring the man who pushed me deliberately. They wouldn't let me through, faces turned twisted and sneering, they swore at me. I was hemmed in, my throat tightened with rising panic. PC Benson spotted me and forced his way through to meet me.

'I've got water,' I yelled.

He heard me and managed to forge a pathway through the mob to meet me by shouting, 'Clear the way, let us through, mind your backs, move back.' People moved aside slowly and with great reluctance but they did actually let us past. The water slopped over the edge of the bucket and drenched my legs and feet. I reached PC Benson and he took it from me, pushed back towards the house and hurled it at the fire. The flames parted and some died, it looked as though the remaining ones were dwindling as the petrol was consumed.

He handed me back the bucket and I went for more. A woman turned to me her face bright with spite. 'Nigger lover, slag, fuck off you nigger lover.'

Doyle spoke into a megaphone. 'Clear the area, clear the area now.'

The crowd fell about shouting and swearing. One of the Brennan twins climbed up on a car further down the road, pulled down his jeans and bared his bum at the police. I saw Doyle use his radio again.

Mr Poole handed me a watering-can and I passed him the bucket. 'Can't find anything else.'

I struggled back with the watering can. The surface of the door was cracked and distorted and the frame charred but it had stopped burning. The flames were still licking up below the lounge window but I could get near enough to pour water over the plywood which was beginning to smoke. A stone smacked against the wall beside me and as I turned another hit above my head with a crack. A ripple of outrage made my cheeks burn.

I crouched and ran to the police car.

Johnny sat there grim faced. I thought about the camera but reasoned that with two police as witnesses to all that was going on they wouldn't need a video as well. The crowd began to clap, faster and faster and to shout something I couldn't make out. Would this have happened if Mandy hadn't been sick? If the council had acted more quickly?

There was a roar from someone and then a battery of bottles, lumps of wood, half-bricks and clods of earth came over. A whoosh and a thump which rocked my belly as a petrol-bomb exploded against the upstairs window, glass shattered and the pane collapsed in. Immediately after another hit the roof washing flames across the tiles. Other things were thrown at the window, one looked like a lump of burning cloth, it reached the curtains of the bed-room and they flared alight.

A beat. Nothing moved but the tongues of fire. I froze. Boom! The thump of the explosion blew away the remnants of the curtain and fragments and glass and lit the window in a flash of intense light. Strips of blackened curtain, dripping with flames, billowed down to the ground.

'Jesus,' shouted Carl. He ran up to the front door and began to lunge against it, using his shoulder. Three or four times and it didn't budge.

He looked back at PC Doyle. 'Come on,' he yelled.

Doyle looked spooked. His cocky assurance unsteadied by the savage turn of events. 'The brigade'll be here any minute,' he shouted. 'Leave it, Bennie. They'll sort it out, they've got the apparatus.'

'There's three kids in there,' I told him, 'you can't just leave them.'

Doyle turned away, huddled over his radio and talked urgently into it. Carl Benson looked stricken. He hurled himself at the door again to no avail. Out of the corner of my eye I saw Johnny slipping out of the passenger door of the police car. I thought he was making a run for it. But he was risking a lot with the mob so close. I willed him to get away safely. Doyle couldn't see him. Another brick hitting the house distracted me, more followed, they were aiming at Carl Benson now. He put his hands up to protect his face.

'Try the back,' I yelled and ran after him round the side of the house to the back garden. I slipped on the way, my shoes full of water. My fake glasses fell off and I cracked them with my hand as I landed. I felt someone grab my arm and turned, ready to wrestle free, but it was Johnny.

'Y'alright?'

'Yes,' I struggled to me feet.

The garden was unkempt, overgrown grass and brambles, silvered in the strong moonlight, caught at our feet as we hurried after Carl. The hoarse screams and cat-calls of the crowd were muffled too but their message of hatred was all too clear. Smoke plumed up from the roof and drifted our way but otherwise there was no sign of the fire. Carl kicked at the door, three or four times. He ran back and Johnny had a go too. My teeth were clenched together tight as I willed the lock to give. They took turns kicking and shouldering it and finally the wood split across and the frame splintered. Another kick from Carl and the door skewed off its hinges and fell dangling at the side of the entrance.

There was darkness within. We stepped directly into the kitchen. I could smell the sharp fumes of petrol and oily smoke. I braced myself for the sound of screams or cries but heard nothing beyond the roaring of the fire upstairs and popping and banging sounds. Where were they? Oh, God, where were they?

Carl rushed ahead. 'Carl, wait,' I yelled but he paid no attention. I grabbed Johnny's shoulder. 'Wait,' I repeated. The sink was by me and there were thin cotton curtains at the window. I ripped these down and turned the tap full on, soaking them and myself into the bargain. I shoved one at Johnny and tied the other round my nose and mouth. I pulled off the wig first, the false hair was slippery and I wanted the cloth to stay on.

There was an explosion then, loud and shocking, and a short scream. I didn't know where Carl had gone. Johnny set off down the hall that led to the stairs. There were two rooms off it. I could just see the doors in the gloom. I opened each and called inside. No movement, no answer. I couldn't see but I knew I shouldn't turn the lights on. Were they in there but hiding from us? Thinking we were the ones out to get them? I tried to listen, to sense if anyone was crouching silent below a table or behind the couch. Where are you? My mind screamed and my heart raced in my chest. I found the bottom of the stairs, now I could see flames coming and going on the landing but mainly smoke, rolling in clouds before me. It became dense quickly. I crawled up the stairs keeping as low as I could. My eyes stung and watered,

I felt the smoke locking my throat up. I was drowning. Another explosion sent a ball of flames the length of the landing, briefly illuminating the area. I saw Johnny's trainers disappear into a doorway. The noise was horrendous, and the toxic stench of burning plastic reached me. I tried to follow but I could no longer breathe. My lungs were sticking together, my balance going. I pushed off the wall and tumbled down the stairs. My heart was thundering. I crawled to the back door and gulped in air then returned, holding my breath and I pulled myself up the stairs. Where were they?

I took the first door again, just inside I stumbled over legs. Jeans. Johnny. So hard to see. No air to speak. Heard him choking, vomiting. Pulled at his legs. He shuffled my way. Another sound, a child's cough. In his arms, the toddler. Out the door, we wriggled, slow, painful. Flames nibbled along the carpet, caught at the bottom of my leg, the nylon melting and sticking fast. Johnny yelped. Hurt too. Had to get out, get out fast. Felt for the first stair, yanked us closer, no air. Buzz of darkness at the back of my skull, swimming closer. Pushing Johnny, tumbling down, bump, bump, bump. The child cries. Can't find the door.

Where's the door gone?

'Bennie?'

'Take them out.'

Voices, hands lifting me up.

Outside, gulping for air and there is none. Then a mask on my face and my panic subsides. An ambulance. The people calm and steady. Johnny on a stretcher. The child, on the paramedic's knee, pulling at her oxygen mask, her face streaked black, her clothes thick with soot.

A fireman approaches us, huge in his gear.

'There are others inside?'

I nod. Remove the mask to speak, my voice is pathetic, and I can't say more than a couple of words without coughing. 'There's a baby and a little boy, their mother, and a policeman.'

He thanks me and runs off.

The ambulance was parked beside the police cars, in the middle of the road. I sat just inside, the back doors were open. The crowd had melted away. Neighbours remained, worried faces, sharing cigarettes and quiet conversations, coats pulled tight. I could see Darren, his face upset and wobbly standing beside his mother.

The moon was glorious, high, bright as neon.

Someone touched my arm. Mr Poole.

'You OK?' His eyes glistened.

I nodded. Clamped my mouth tight to hold the tears.

One of the engines was running foam into the upstairs window. A second ambulance arrived. The crew began to get out stretchers and blankets.

'We'll be off in a minute,' the paramedic said. 'Take you for a check at the A&E, get those burns dressed.' The child on her lap whimpered. I reached across and stroked her back. Apart from the filth of the fire she appeared unhurt.

'Is he OK?' I croaked, meaning Johnny.

'Yes, he'll be fine. There's burns to his arm and his side, we keep him lying down so there's less stress on the injuries.'

'The bastards,' I whispered.

'You know, when the fire brigade arrived they stoned them. Want shooting, whole bloody lot of them,' she said.

More police had arrived and a few of them clustered round the patrol cars. I could see PC Doyle, hands on hip looking this way and that as though he was lost and Carl Benson's partner talking to a colleague and gesturing angrily.

Johnny turned and raised himself up on

267

one elbow. I saw his jaw tighten but he disguised the pain pretty well. What made him so brave? There he was, under arrest by a bigoted cop, surrounded by a mob of racists and rather than sneak off and drive away he'd dived into a burning house. 'They got them?' he asked.

The paramedic climbed out the van, the child in her arms. 'There's someone coming out now.'

I strained to see. A cluster of firemen emerged from the side of the house carrying a stretcher chair bearing Mrs Ahmed with an oxygen mask over her face. She was wrapped in a blanket, she had nothing on her feet, the scarf on her head was blackened. They brought her to the ambulance beside ours. She was completely dazed. I could see now that she clutched her baby to her chest.

'We need to look at the baby, see if he's alright,' one of the ambulance crew knelt crouched down to try and get to the infant. I stared. There was no movement. The baby's dead, I thought. She knew it and she didn't want to admit it yet. A ball of emotion clogged my throat. Then the baby stirred, its head shifted to the side and it gave a harsh cough. The paramedic sat back on his heels and released the breath he'd been holding.

'We'll just give him some oxygen too, that's it, lift his head.' Mrs Ahmed didn't respond. She sat passively while they set up the baby's mask. The toddler spotted her mother and wriggled in the paramedic's arms. She talked gently to the child who only cried louder.

The toddler cried again, holding her hands out for her mother. The woman took her over. The little girl stood to the side of the chair, put her head in her mother's lap. Mrs Ahmed moved one hand from the baby to rest on her daughter's head but she continued to gaze into the distance.

'The baby's doing remarkably well,' said one of the paramedics to his colleague, 'but I don't like the look of the mother.'

'We can take all these in now,' said the woman, including the Ibrahims along with Johnny and I.

'What about the little boy?' I asked. 'And Carl, the policeman.'

'We don't know,' she said.

'Please, can you find out?'

She walked over to one of the firemen and they talked for a couple of moments. I exchanged glances with Mr Poole who waited beside me. I saw the stretchers being taken round to the house.

She came back, her face solemn. 'I'm sorry,' she said, 'the lads did all they could.'

In the silence that followed I heard the roar of denial deafening in my ears, felt the swell of despair surge up from the guts, my scalp grow taut, my head swim. I moved the mask aside, covered my eyes with my good hand and let the tears leak out. That little boy. No. Oh God, no. And Carl, who'd given his life trying to save him. A good lad, Mr Poole had called him. A good lad. Not the sort you came across often enough in the police force. Johnny lay back on the stretcher and closed his eyes tight. Mr Poole placed his hand on my shoulder and squeezed.

'I'm sorry,' I spoke to Mrs Ahmed a little later, 'your boy.' She was oblivious, in deep shock. She must have known already. She sat still as stone, one hand stroking the little girl's hair, the other still enfolding her baby.

I turned to Mr Poole, 'And Carl…'

He shook his head, his soft jowls trembling with the motion, he rubbed at his face with his hands.

'We couldn't see anything, it was so confusing, the smoke and the noise. I didn't know where any of them were. If I'd known which room…'

'You did everything you could,' said Mr Poole. 'Just like Carl. He didn't have to go in there, none of you did. People will remember him for that.'

'A hero?' My voice wobbled dangerously. 'I'd rather he was alive.'

'Of course, so would I. "Happy the land that has no heroes",' he quoted. 'But if Carl had made it maybe they wouldn't have,' he gestured towards the woman and her children. 'He did his job, more than his job. When I talk to his mother that's what I'll tell her, that he was the best, his humanity took him in there, into that fire. He cared. It's right to be proud of that.'

I was glad that Mr Poole knew Carl's mother and would be able to describe to her all the events of that night, tell the story over and over, answer her questions. And Mrs Ahmed, who would talk with her? With a jolt I remembered her husband.

'Mr Ibrahim! They must get him, tell him. He's at work.'

Someone called a policeman over and I told him about Mr Ibrahim, my words punctuated by coughing. 'It's in Chorlton somewhere.'

'Heaven's Bridge,' supplied Mr Poole, 'High Lane.'

'Thanks, we'll get someone round there.'

Gradually we were seated in the ambulance, Mr Poole retrieved my bag for me and several different people made notes of our names and addresses.

Then they closed up the doors and as we drove away I could see the house through the small window, door charred, the blackened window frames gaping in the dark. The fresh graffiti on the wall still visible: 'Nigger bastards go home'.

Chapter Twenty

We made the journey in silence. I began to feel unbearably cold and started to shiver, my wet feet had gone numb and my leg ached fiercely.

At the hospital we were all seen by the triage nurses and split off into different cubicles. I was shaky and nauseous but I managed to use the payphone to ring home, thankful when Sheila answered. In a breathy croak I told her I was at the hospital, that something had come up with work and I wasn't sure when I'd get home. Her interest and warmth brought me close to crying again so I kept the call brief.

I returned to my cubicle and reclined on the trolley. I was freezing and asked for another blanket but nothing ever materialised. Time seemed frozen, too. I read all the dilapidated notices about correct use of the equipment in the room and studied the sellotape marks on the walls.

I became familiar with the moans from the woman across the way who had stomach pain and kept vomiting and with the persistent outbursts from an exasperated old woman who wanted only to go home. Beside her sat an incredibly young care-worker who spoke occasionally to tell her she could go home once she'd seen the doctor. I'd passed the pair of them on the way to the phone, sitting side by side and looking like they'd just landed in purgatory.

At lengthy intervals nurses and doctors came in and made notes, asked questions, took blood samples, asked me to breathe into tubes, dressed my leg, gave me a leaflet and a note for my GP's practice nurse and at long, long, last told me I could go home.

I sought out Johnny and found him in one

of the bays. They'd covered his burns but he was to get the dressings changed daily as they were worried about the risk of infection.

'They cut my Levi jacket up, you know,' he feigned outrage, 'and my Joe Bloggs shirt.'

I tried to smile but I felt lousy and I'm sure it looked pathetic. 'I can probably get you some money for it, claim it from the council when I bill them. Oh, and I owe you the cab fare.'

'Forget it.'

'Does it hurt?'

'Kills but they've given us some really strong tablets. Need 'em, I can tell you.'

'Look, that policeman, the one who arrested you, Doyle, if he tries to follow it up…'

'I'll sue him for wrongful arrest. My cousin's a lawyer, he's good he is. And my uncle.'

'I think he'll forget about it, after what happened. You saving the little girl.'

He looked sheepish.

'But if he does try anything, I'll be a witness. It was racial harassment, he was totally out of order. The police will want to see us anyway, about the fire. It's murder now. I know who was behind it and so do they.

There'll be a trial.'

'And seeing as one of their own's dead, they'll have to take it seriously for a change.'

His scepticism was well-placed. It wasn't all that long since the Chief Constable had admitted to institutional racism in his own force in the wake of the Stephen Lawrence inquiry.

'Shame it was one of the good ones,' I added.

'Yeah. Should have been that other joker.' He shifted on his seat, settled his bandaged arm again. 'One of my cousins went in the police, he was determined he was going to make a go of it. Fast track promotion, all that, he was a graduate and you know how they're always going on about needing more black and Asian officers... We all thought he was tapped. Anyway, he lasted eight months. Nearly destroyed him. They were all like that Doyle, or worse. Stories he told me. Sick. Like that lot. Setting a house on fire, burning children.'

'And...' sudden tears caught me un-awares. I fought to swallow them, wiped at my eyes with my hand. 'I keep remembering him,' I said, 'the little boy. I only saw him once, he translated for his mum.' I had to break off again. I took a deep breath or two.

'How old was he?'

'Six, seven? I feel so angry, at what they've done. And I feel so bloody useless too. It's like "what can I do?" What can anybody do? What will actually change anything?'

I wasn't expecting answers from Johnny and he didn't offer any. We sat quietly for a little while lost in thought.

'How are you getting home?' I broke the silence. 'And your car!'

'My Dad's coming for me. He's gonna drop my brother off to get the car. We share it.'

'Who chose the seat covers?'

'Eh?'

'The leopard print?'

'Why?'

I shook my head. 'Doesn't matter.'

'No, go on. What's wrong with them?'

'Nothing. Look, thank you, what you did, going in there. It was brilliant.'

'Yeah,' he looked embarrassed, 'you didn't do so bad yourself, wet curtains and all.'

I smiled. 'Improvise. I want to see the Ibrahims before I go.'

'They were down at the end before.'

I got to my feet. 'I'll see you, then. Take care.'

'Yeah. See you.'

I went looking but the end bays were deserted. I asked the triage nurse.

'You've just missed them, I think.'

'Have they been admitted?'

'No, no. They're OK. They've sorted out some emergency accommodation for them. You might just catch them, they've only just gone.'

I pushed through the swing doors and down the ramp of the ambulance bay where a clutch of smokers hovered.

I saw the family a few yards down the path walking away, a policeman and a woman with them.

I caught them up.

'Mr Ibrahim?' He turned quickly, the toddler in his arms, a frown on his face. The others stopped.

'I'm sorry, about your little boy, please tell your wife. I'm so sorry.'

I glanced at her, she looked at me blankly, then shifted the baby closer to her shoulder.

'You were one of the people who went into the house?' he asked.

'Yes.'

'Thank you.'

I didn't want his thanks. 'I've been working for the council,' I explained, 'filming for evidence.'

He studied me for a moment. 'Now they have their evidence.'

I swallowed. I didn't say anything.

'They should never have left us there, you tell your council people that.'

I nodded.

He turned and they walked on.

Back in the Casualty department I rang for a black cab and was thankful, when it arrived, to get a taciturn driver. He never even commented on how I smelt.

I needed a bath. I knew it wasn't a sociable thing to do at that hour in the morning but I was desperate to wash away the soot and the acrid stench of smoke and it would be easier to keep my bandages dry in a bath rather than a shower. First I made a cup of tea and took it up. I had a sudden rush of anxiety about Maddie and Tom and went in to look at them. They were both sleeping peacefully and I left before I could become too maudlin. I put a towel in the bath to try and muffle the noise but it didn't help much and did nothing to quieten the gurgling of the pipes.

I heard Ray calling my name. I stopped the taps and opened the bathroom door.

He began to complain, blinking in the

light, running his hand through his unruly hair. Then he got a look at me.

'Oh, God. What's happened?'

I opened my mouth then snapped it shut, pressed my fingers to my lips. That set off the shakes, everything began to tremble. I shook my head at him then my control caved in and I began to bawl like a baby.

He led me downstairs and into the kitchen. Made me tea without asking, handed me the kitchen roll. He quizzed me about my injuries, wanted to know what the hospital had done, whether I'd be OK, how I was feeling and of course how I'd got hurt.

In little bursts and puffs I told him about the tragedies of the night. When I reached the part about the firemen not being able to save the little Ibrahim boy and Carl Benson, I began to cry noisily again and with all the artlessness of fresh grief. 'It's awful, it's so awful, why should they be dead?' I ranted. 'It's not fair. That little boy… And it's not just that either, there's you and Laura as well. I don't know how we'll manage if you move out. I'll miss Tom so much and if you take Digger too Maddie will be heart-broken.'

'Hang on, hang on. Who said I was moving out?'

I blew my nose but it was impossible to breathe through it anymore. 'No-one, but it's obviously a very serious relationship and it's going to affect us all. If you get married or...'

Children even. There was another whole area to fret about. If Laura wanted children, oh God.

'...well, even if you just live together.'

'Sal!'

I jumped. 'Yes?'

'Is this what you wanted to talk about on Tuesday?'

'Sort of, yes.'

'Laura and I haven't even talked about any of this sort of stuff. We've only been going out a few months.'

'But it's so intense.' I protested.

'Don't you think I'd have talked to you if I was considering anything like that? Taking Tom and leaving? You're talking about massive changes.'

'I know.'

I must have looked pathetic because Ray didn't pursue this 'what sort of a bastard do you think I am' line. He just did some sort of Italian shimmy with his hands and muttered some curse I couldn't translate.

'Watch my lips. Laura and I have no plans

to live together, get married, elope or do a runner. Who knows where the relationship will go. But *if* we even begin to talk about anything like that you will know, I promise.'

I swallowed.

'Now you'd better go get that bath. I'm off to bed. I can take and collect the kids tomorrow.'

'Thanks,' I left the room before I could lose it again.

The water turned dirty grey as I washed, an oily film floated on the surface. It was laborious getting in and out without wetting my dressing, lying with my bad leg up on the side of the bath. The pain returned in my leg and I took two more tablets before I went to bed.

I slept badly. There were bones in my pillow and ashes in my mouth and a small boy in Batman pyjamas flew wheeling and swooping through my dreams...

Chapter Twenty One

The pain was the first thing I was aware of when I woke up. It was chewing up the bone in my leg. I took two tablets and lay back, trying to place the snapshots in my mind in some sort of sequence. I went over the events of the previous night twice, from getting in Johnny's taxi to crying in the kitchen. Then I did my best to blank it out.

I must have been in shock or after-shock. Certainly some altered state which re-ordered all my priorities and which explains, if anything can, what I did that day. Everything was dream-like. Everything was in the distance. I couldn't concentrate on the unessentials but I was completely focussed on the task I set myself.

After breakfast I tried to get my bike out but the burn soon protested. I wouldn't be able to pedal the thing even if I could get up onto the saddle. I rang a cab and asked them to pick me up from the Dobson's address in half-an-hour.

I walked round there slowly. I was cold

even though the weather was mild. I collected my small tape-recorder from the filing cabinet and checked the tape and batteries. Fine. I was glad I didn't have to struggle changing batteries one-handed. I put the recorder in my jacket pocket.

The little mosaic vase stood on the cabinet. I picked it up and ran my thumb over the smooth, glass tiles. I thought of Jennifer in her dry, dusty grave, of Carl's mother, answering her door to a policeman, knowing the news before he spoke, of Mrs Ahmed aching for the feel of her son's hand in hers, for the light in his eyes. I placed the ornament down carefully and locked up.

I sat back in the cab and let my mind roam. When the taxi drew up to the kerb I felt my stomach tense. I paid the fare and watched him drive away.

I rang the bell, a long push, heard it shrilling inside the house and then the sound of movements, the voice at the door.

'Who is it?' Cautious. Most people open the door without asking.

'Children of Christ.'

'Just a minute,' the chain rattled then she let me in.

'Come in, in here,' she led me into her room.

I switched the tape-recorder on.

She settled in her chair. I sat on the edge of the bed. She looked at me expectantly. I stared back. Her smile faltered and behind the glasses her eyes hardened as she became alert to the possibility of subterfuge.

'You're not from the church.'

'No. I came the other day, about Jennifer.'

'Get out of my house,' she began to stand up.

'No.' I didn't raise my voice but I made it clear I wasn't budging. 'I want to know the truth. It's important to me.'

'You've no right.'

'Oh, I think I have. I know what happened to Jennifer, you see. Most of it.'

Expressions flashed across her face; apprehension, outrage, uncertainty.

'Get out,' she repeated, 'if you don't leave now...'

'What will you do? Call the police? They might be interested in the truth as well.'

'I don't know what you're talking about,' she blustered, 'I won't talk to you.'

'Alright, you listen then. I'll tell you all about it, about Jennifer. She was a bright girl, got a place at university. Worked hard but she still knew how to enjoy herself, she had some good friends, they speak very

284

warmly of her. She worked too, waitressing, earning money of her own.

'She finished school in 1976. She was due to go to Keele that autumn, she'd got a place studying English, as long as she got her grades. Everyone knew she would. It was a long, hot summer. They declared a drought. Jennifer spent it working at the Bounty, but she got away too, she and Lisa went off to Knebworth, a pop festival. They had a brilliant time. She told you she was going camping.'

Mrs Pickering sat with her head turned away from me, facing the window. From what I could see her face was impassive. Her hands were tightly clasped in her lap.

'But Jennifer never arrived at Keele. She never left home, did she? She couldn't.'

In the pause there was the faint wheeze of her breath and from the outside the shrieks and laughter of a school playtime.

'She went to Keele.'

'No, she didn't. You know that's a lie.'

'She went to Keele.'

'She didn't,' I raised my voice. 'She never went there. I've spoken to the university, she was never admitted. She never left here.'

'She ran away,' she retorted. 'We thought she'd gone there. Maybe it was somewhere else. She ran away.'

'And later that year you invented the story that Jennifer had dropped out of university?'

She hesitated, caught in the web she'd spun, desperately trying to work out whether agreement or denial would best fit her new version of events where Jennifer was a runaway. That moment's pause removed any last shreds of doubt I had about my suspicions.

'She didn't run away,' I said plainly. 'She'd have been better off if she had. There was a big row. I can't be sure exactly who said what and in what order, but it probably went something like this. Jennifer was pregnant, she told you and your husband. He was appalled, wasn't he? You both were but with his position in the church to consider, his failure to maintain high moral standards in his own home – well, he'd be beside himself.'

Mrs Pickering was shaking her head as if to ward off a troublesome wasp. She refused to look at me.

'What did he do? Demand to know who the father was? Did she tell? That won't have helped matters; he was a black boy she'd been seeing. Your husband would have found that hard to stomach, with his racist beliefs. The relationship had finished so marriage would have been out of the question for Jennifer. Did he threaten to disinherit her, denounce her? Or maybe he told her a secret of his own. That she was no daughter of his, that she'd been illegitimate. Bad blood will out. Something like that?'

Her head jerked back at this but still she kept her own counsel. I kept right on. 'He was shouting, her lack of decency, her shameless behaviour. Probably used a few choice words from the scriptures. There's plenty in there isn't there? Whores of Babylon and the like. But Jennifer had discovered something about Frank, a secret of her own. Maybe she flung that back at him. Knocked him off the moral high ground. Or was that what started the row? Did she tell you about his sins before she got onto hers? You know what I'm talking about?'

Mrs Pickering was completely still, her hands gripping each other, her mouth pressed into a line.

'He'd been having an affair with Marjorie Shuttle.'

'No. No.' Her hoarse denial rang out.

'I've been to see Mrs Shuttle, she told me all about it. So, he tried to silence Jennifer, to stop her saying all those vile things. Perhaps he pushed her, punched her. He was a big man.'

'No,' she began to moan, a guttural sound from deep inside.

I thought uneasily of her frail health. Was I hounding her to total collapse? But I was so near; her silence and her reactions told me that my story was close enough to the events of that fateful summer. I wanted her to own the truth.

'He killed her,' I said baldly, 'and then he buried her in the garden. He put a new shed over the grave.'

'No, no,' she kept repeating, rocking forward slightly in her chair.

'The ground was hard as iron, it'd been baking for months. All that effort; the digging, building, it made him ill. That and the guilt. It broke his heart, shredded his nerves. I'm right.'

'No,' she said violently, twisting my way but avoiding my eyes.

'Why are you protecting him?' I leant forward. 'He'd dead too. Nothing can hurt him now. He's dead. Jennifer is dead and he is dead and he killed her.'

She looked then. Her face naked with emotion, her eyes wounded and the scales fell from my own. I was astonished. A shudder of realisation ran up my spine.

'You did it.'

There was no denial.

'He was protecting you, not the other way round.'

She turned to the window. 'It...' she faltered.

I stayed completely still. The hairs on my arms and the back of my neck prickled. I waited. It was quieter outside, playtime over. Just the to and fro of traffic and a dog barking in the distance.

'Accident,' she whispered.

Another silence. I didn't speak, didn't break the spell. She might clam up. I was so close. But if the silence stretched too far the moment may be lost. I counted to five.

'An accident,' I prompted.

'The things she said. Hurtful, sinful lies. He was a good man. The filth... I was ironing. I didn't mean to ... it was in my hand. I told her to stop it. Stop it. Stop it. She wouldn't. I hit her with it. On the head, in the face. I only meant her to be quiet.' She raised her palms and pressed her fingertips to her mouth, closed her eyes. I felt some compassion for her then. The burden of her secret held for years, the loss of her daughter and then her husband. How strong she must have been to carry on, to never weaken. Never allowing herself to grieve for Jennifer, twisting her memory into that of a feckless girl who had jettisoned her family. Had she loved her? Had she ever defended her bright, young daughter to her husband? Or had Jennifer always been the cuckoo child, a reminder of hidden sin, of bad blood? Her independent spirit seen as waywardness, her presence a cross to bear not a precious gift? Had either of them ever given her a hug in those awkward teenage years, ever pulled her close with affection? Oh, Jennifer.

She straightened up, returned her hands to her lap, her eyes were dry. 'She did it to spite us, you know. Going with a coloured boy. It made me feel sick.'

She pursed her lips and I was reminded of the look on Caroline Cunningham's face when she discussed Lisa MacNeice's lesbianism.

'My daughter in bed with a nigger, carrying his child. Dirty. Loathsome. She had to spoil everything. After all Frank had done, taking us in, giving her his name. We moved here so people wouldn't talk. She grew up and she was a snake in the grass.

He had to put up with her bad manners and her cheap ideas. She had no respect. She was a slut. And then to tell such terrible lies about him, foul-mouthed lies.'

'It was an accident,' I said. 'Why didn't you get an ambulance?'

'We couldn't tell anyone,' she shook her head. 'All the fuss. With Frank at the Church and his firm. It would have ruined him.'

It did anyway.

'And there was Roger. He doesn't have to know?' she pleaded.

What was she asking me to do? Keep her secret? Say nothing?

'He wanted to find his sister.'

'But not this.'

'No, not this.'

'You won't tell him?' Her voice was soft.

I couldn't speak.

'And the police?'

She wouldn't stand trial. She'd be dead before any case could be heard. She was no danger to anyone now. But I'd come for the truth and I couldn't give her the assurances she demanded.

'I'm sorry,' I told her.

Her face fell, fatigue pinching at it. 'Please, could you get me a glass of water?'

She cleared her throat.

I went along to the kitchen, fished in the cupboards for a glass and ran the water. Outside I could see the shed, Jennifer's tomb. How could her mother have borne the memories of her death and what followed? Keeping the body hidden from Roger while they sorted out buying the shed, digging the pit, bringing her from the house, wrapped in a sheet or a rug. Burying her. Laying the floor of the shed on top. Did they pray for her? Or was she beyond redemption? Did the sin of murder mean they could no longer offer prayers? Would their God forgive or punish? How long before they'd cleared her room? Removing her posters, the troll in the window, her make-up, her diaries, her precious mementoes.

Then each time a friend rang up or a neighbour inquired the gorge of fear that must have reared up. Lisa MacNeice trying to report her missing, Mrs Clerkenwell asking about her, Roger wanting to find her. Roger who was so disappointed that he never got to wave his big sister off at the train station. No chance to say goodbye. Like the Ibrahims; sudden death, no chance to say goodbye. Tiredness rolled over me, my leg was aching again. I should go. I carried the water into the hall.

Mrs Pickering stood at the end, framed in the light from the glass in the door. She was holding a gun, one with a long barrel. It was pointing straight at me. Her finger was on the trigger...

Chapter Twenty Two

I had an inappropriate urge to giggle. Fear does that. The glass in my hand was shaking, water spilling over the side. Where the hell had she got a gun from? Did she know how to use it? I knew next to nothing about guns but whatever sort it was, she'd be bound to hit me at this range. She would barely need to aim the thing.

'You won't tell Roger.'

'What you going to do, kill me too?' I said hoarsely. 'If you shoot me it'll all come out anyway.'

'Why should it?' She was hard now, the shutters clamped down on the memories I'd dug up. 'You entered my house under false pretences. When you refused to leave I defended myself. I have a right to defend my property.'

'There are notes,' I said, 'in my files. The police would have to investigate.'

'But you thought Frank did it.' She wasn't stupid.

I reckoned there was about twenty feet between us. The gun was pointing at my middle. My mind was racing round hunting for a way out. The pain in my leg was smouldering again, diminishing my ability to think straight, act clever.

Unexpectedly her face creased, the colour drained swiftly away and beads of sweat broke out on her forehead and upper lip as the onslaught of pain racked her. It was the first glimpse I had seen of the savagery of her disease. The barrel of the gun wavered and she fought to level it at me again.

'Another killing won't help. It's too late.'

'Why can't you let it be?' she gasped.

'Jennifer. I think she deserved it. The truth should be known.'

'What good will it do? The truth will only hurt Roger. It will destroy him.'

'I hope not.' But there were no guarantees.

The pain tore at her again. She froze, her face a mask of agony.

'Can I get you anything, tablets?' Before

you kill me. She blinked a refusal.

I weighed up the possibilities of escaping from the line of fire. If I ran back into the kitchen I might be able to get out the back door, if it was open. What if it was locked, would the key be there? Or there was the back room ahead a little to my left. Then what? Break a window, clamber out. In either case she could follow and shoot me. I didn't want her to fire the gun. I didn't dare make any sudden moves. I'd no idea how fast her reactions would be. And I didn't want to die. Oh, God I didn't want to die. What about Maddie? I couldn't leave Maddie. My knee was trembling uncontrollably, and my hands still shaking, drops of water continued to spill over the edge of the glass and drip from my hand. I'd have to talk her round.

She swayed, her arms jerking as she struggled to keep the gun steady.

'This is ridiculous,' I said. 'Give me the gun.'

She shot me.

The noise was stupendous and the hall clouded with smoke and the smell of fireworks. I was on the floor. Smoke. I saw Carl running into the Ibrahims' house, Mrs Ahmed clutching her baby tight, me thinking it was dead. Jennifer was dead, her baby was dead. The little boy was dead. My left arm, my shoulder were screaming in agony. Lumps of plaster littered the ground around me and dust mingled with the smoke. The sound of the shot still roared in my ears.

The force of the discharge had thrown her to the floor. She'd dropped the gun. I shuffled along the hall on my good side. The piercing pains shot through my arm and made me whimper. I stretched for the gun with my undamaged hand and pulled it beside me. I looked back to the kitchen. Her aim had gone wide, holes had ripped into the top of the door frame, the wall and ceiling. Big holes. Were there any holes like that in me? I felt giddy with apprehension.

She lay there, her breathing harsh and torn. She wore sheepskin slippers. I sat for a few moments propped against the wall and tried to gather some strength. I thought about home, about Maddie, hold on I told myself, get up, get out. I struggled to my feet, the pain surged in my leg making me dizzy. The gun weighed a ton, I took it into the kitchen and put it on the table.

I made my way slowly down the passageway and stooped over her. The smoke scratched at my throat and made me cough.

My heart was still thumping wildly in my chest, the adrenaline making all my senses taut. She'd shot me. The woman had shot me. She could have killed me for fuck's sake.

I tried to get her into a sitting position; she was shivering and her eyes were empty and fixed on something only she could see.

'Mrs Pickering?'

There was no response. I could still hear her breath see her chest moving. Saliva trickled from one corner of her mouth, her face looked lopsided, she held one arm rigid against her body. A stroke? I struggled to lay her down again in the recovery position. Crying out as the pain ripped my arm.

The dogs next door were going apeshit, presumably all their hunting race-memories awakened by the gunshot. There was hammering on the front door as well.

I went and opened it. Mrs Clerkenwell. 'Hello, I heard an awful... Blimey.' She spotted Mrs Pickering.

'It's alright. An accident. But Mrs Pickering is very upset. She's in shock I think. I'm going to call an ambulance. Ring Roger. Could you come and sit with her while I sort things out?'

'Yes, of course. What on earth happened?'

'An accident, with a gun.'

'A gun! Oh, dear. Right. I'll just lock up at mine.'

I shut the door and turned to Mrs Pickering. She looked awful, pale and her face slack.

I dialled 999. Gave all the details and even had the presence of mind to ask where they would take her. Then I rang Roger.

Roger was confused and anxious when I spoke to him. Not surprising really as I was giving a highly edited version of exactly what had happened. I told him that I'd called for a second interview with his mother, that she'd become upset, that her gun had gone off and she was badly shocked. I wasn't sure whether she had suffered a stroke.

'A stroke! Oh, no. And her gun! What the old shotgun? Oh, God. Oh, I am sorry. I thought it was in the cellar. She'll kill someone with that one day. Farm mentality. Shoot first, ask questions later. She probably thought you were an intruder or something.'

'Mmmm. Look, I don't want to leave it here, I'll take it with me. Mrs Clerkenwell's coming over to wait for the ambulance with me.'

'Oh, God,' he said. 'And are you alright?'

'Fine,' I lied and was immediately rewarded with a swirl of anxiety.

'You didn't say you wanted to see my mother again, I could have warned her.'

'Yes. I know. But with her being so unhappy about my enquiries I didn't think she'd agree to see me if she had any choice. I decided to just call on spec, give it a second go.'

'And she got the old gun out. Oh, what a mess. And you think it might be a stroke? Is she going to be alright?'

'I don't know. It could just be shock, but her mouth's all pulled down at one side. There's an ambulance on the way, they'll know or the hospital. You're probably best going straight there. To M.R.I. We've our meeting fixed for Monday but I'll talk to you before then. Let me know how she is.'

'Yes, I will. Erm ... there's no good news, then? Mother didn't say anything...'

Oh, heck. 'No, there isn't. I'm sorry.'

It wasn't the time or the place to reveal to Roger the tragedy of Jennifer's disappearance and part of me wondered whether in the intervening days Mrs Pickering might tell him herself, if she was able to speak.

'And this business with the gun,' he

stumbled over the words, 'you won't ... will you report it ... the police?'

'No, I'm not going to report it.' Not that.

'I am sorry,' he repeated. 'What was she doing? Of all the stupid things.'

'Let me know how she is, won't you.'

'Yes. I'll see you on Monday.'

I put the gun in a bin liner from the kitchen. I sat down and looked at my arm. There were holes in my jacket and fleece top and blood soaking through the patches. Not obvious from a distance as I was wearing my black jacket so the blood didn't show much. I could feel it warm and sticky and it was running down my hand in little rivulets. I wiped it clean with a tea-towel which I chucked in the bin. The pain from my burn actually felt worse than the throbbing in my arm, except when I moved it, then I had to breathe through it – like they teach you for childbirth. I couldn't face Casualty again. I'd try and clear it up myself and see the GP if that failed. I'd had a tetanus jab not all that long ago so hopefully I'd be protected from lock-jaw. If it was a real mess I'd get myself along to the hospital. But there was no way I was going in then with Mrs Pickering and a lot of tricky questions to answer.

Mrs Clerkenwell knocked at the door again and I let her in. The hall reeked of gunsmoke. She coughed and covered her mouth.

'Gun powder,' I explained.

'Where on earth did she get a gun?'

'It was an old shotgun, came from when they had the farm.'

'Oh, heavens,' her eyes widened with concern and she lowered her voice, 'she wasn't, you know, trying to … if the pain got too much.'

I laughed. I could still laugh. 'No, nothing like that. But she needs to get to hospital. I don't know whether it's just shock or whether she's had a stroke of some sort.'

'Well, what on earth was she doing?' She stooped down beside Mrs Pickering who lay with her eyes closed, her breathing regular.

Trying to kill me. 'She thought I was an intruder, just a stupid mix-up.'

'Did she fire it at you?' She said appalled. 'Yes, your arm. Oh, good heavens.'

'I'm fine. Nothing broken. Just a few cuts. Most of it ended up in the ceiling.' I wanted to get out of there away from her questions. I felt fragile as though I might dissolve if I had to stand about much longer. I limped over to lean on the wall.

'And your leg!'

'That didn't happen here. It's a long story.'

The ringing of the doorbell signified the arrival of the ambulance. I gave them a quick resume of events. Glances were exchanged when the gun was mentioned but I told them it was an accident. I had to give my name and address in case anyone needed to follow it up and I told them that Roger, her next of kin was on his way to the hospital. Once the facts were established they wasted no time in strapping her onto a stretcher and taking her away.

I rang a taxi immediately after.

'Are you sure you're going to be alright?' Mrs Clerkenwell asked.

'Yes. I just need to get home.'

'You might be better getting someone to look at that arm.'

'I will,' I said. 'If it's not a cream and plaster job I'll get it seen to.'

'It's a good job you had that coat on. I mean look at the state of the place.'

I looked. The dust had settled but the splintered wood and pockmarked plaster showed where most of the shot had ended up. And if she hadn't been so weak, if her aim had been surer, if the gun hadn't kicked her back at that particular angle, it could have been my face, my eyes.

A car horn sounded.

'That'll be my cab. I expect Roger will have a key.'

'Yes. I'll make sure it's locked.' She opened the door. 'All this – it's got something to do with looking for Jennifer hasn't it?'

I gave her a look.

'I know,' she raised her hands in surrender, 'you can't say. Go on then, and be careful with that arm.'

Chapter Twenty Three

I kept my arm bent on the journey so the blood wouldn't drip onto the seats. The dustbin lorry was making its way down my road so I got dropped at the end. I limped home, the rifle in my good hand, wrapped in its black plastic, like some gunfighter from a B-movie. All I needed was High Noon playing in the background or the whistling from The Good, the Bad and the Ugly. I'd never been able to work out the words to that one, always sounded like 'who ate my Lego'.

I didn't feel much like a hero. I was wasted, battered and burnt. There were no townsfolk ready to pat my back and tip their hats. It seemed such a long walk home. And what was there to celebrate? A job well done? I argued to myself that I had done my best, that I had done what I could, that it wasn't my fault that things had turned out so badly. I knew intellectually that my persistence and my wits had led me to uncover the truth about Jennifer. But she was dead, all I could bring her brother was her corpse and a story to shatter his world. As for the Ibrahims, whatever happened to their tormentors they had lost a child. Their son had been murdered. And a young policeman had died with him.

I shuffled past the dustbin lorry, avoiding the men who pulled the wheelie bins onto the automatic fork-lift at the back. My teeth ached in my mouth, my leg was pulsing with pain and my arm was aflame. I felt so sick. My face was wet. Stupid tears. I hadn't any tissues. It was hard to get my key in the lock. I was cold too. I sniffed hard and tried again.

Once inside I used my good arm to push the gun on the high shelf in the hall, as I turned away it slid off and cracked me on

304

the temple, sending a sickening sensation through me and I lost my temper.

'Stupid fucking thing,' I screamed and triggered a coughing fit. I wanted to get hold of it and smash it to bits, bang it on concrete until it was broken and bent but I was too hurt. I pushed it back up, crying with frustration now.

I went upstairs to the bathroom to examine my arm. I eased my jacket off. The tape recorder looked intact. I rewound it and played a fragment. Barely audible. It didn't matter now. I wasn't about to forget what she had said. I took off my fleece and my t-shirt, pausing each time the movements made the pain ripple and made me sway. Several pellets had lodged in my upper arm, one in the shoulder. They looked like bits of gravel. Blood had streamed from each of them and run down to soak my cuffs. Like long ago days, when I'd fallen off my roller skates and pebble-dashed my knees and sat wincing in the kitchen while my mother picked the grit out with tweezers and daubed the lot with sweet smelling Germolene. I collected the first aid kit and made my way gingerly down to the kitchen. I laid it all out on the table. Talking aloud I enumerated all my woes and cursed and swore while I sorted out the essential items and mixed up some disinfectant. I made tea and took two of the painkillers that the hospital had given me. Everything took me twice as long as the injuries made my left hand useless.

My arm was swelling, the pellets sinking deeper into puffy flesh and bruising edging the wounds. It was hot to the touch. I used the tweezers to dig out the bits letting myself howl and moan when it hurt. Which it did. A lot. Some of the fragments were sharp edged and tore at my skin as I pulled. Each wound bled afresh which I hoped would wash out any dirt. At last I thought they were all out. I dabbed disinfectant on the first one and screamed at the bite. I couldn't bear it.

I mixed water from the kettle with salt and used that. That hurt too. Holding my breath I slathered Germolene around the holes and wrapped a large sterile dressing over the area. One-handed I couldn't fasten it as snugly as I wanted, I'd ask Sheila to re-do it later. The huge dressing had been in the first aid box for ages, I'd always wondered why they had included it – it seemed so extreme. Now it had found a home.

In the lounge I poured myself a generous measure of brandy and sat on the sofa with my legs up. I sipped at the drink, the glow fierce in my tongue and warm as it went down my throat to my stomach. I gazed out at the garden, losing myself in the patterns of the tree branches against the sky. The sun edged its way into the garden and in through the large windows, it reached the sofa. I drained the brandy and got the cotton throw off the easy chair, lay down again and covered myself with it.

The sun was warm on my face and chest, amber light through my eyelids. I soaked in the glow as I spiralled into sleep.

I woke with a start. It was three o'clock. For a moment I panicked about picking the kids up until I remembered Ray's assurance that he would do it. The phone was ringing, then the answerphone kicked in.

I sat up, balking at the pain as both my arm and leg protested. My mouth was dry, my tongue like a pumice stone, my throat felt raw. I could hear a man's voice leaving a message. I got to my feet testing my weight on my damaged leg. I could walk if I took it slowly.

I got a glass of water in the kitchen and chugged it down. Digger looked at me expectantly and padded over. His wagging tail thumped against my leg and all the nerve endings shrieked in agony. I gasped aloud and gripped the sink until it felt safe to let go. Digger had slunk back under the table. I chucked him a dog biscuit. No hard feelings.

The light on the answerphone told me there were two messages. I played them back. Diane had heard about the fire, from Ray, and would call round later to see how I was getting on. The second message was from the detectives following up an enquiry into the fire; they would be contacting me for a statement. Good. I wanted those thugs sent down. I wondered whether they had other witnesses; had anyone actually seen who threw the petrol bombs? Could they prosecute them all for involvement, conspiracy to endanger life or whatever? The tapes would help build the case, too. Had Mandy Bellows heard about it all yet? If she'd not been ill would action have been taken already and the fire not happened? If we'd got into the house more quickly, if we could have got in the front? If the police had sent a riot squad instead of two patrol cars? I realised what I was doing and shook my head. All the supposition in the world wouldn't change the facts. Nor would feeling guilty.

I was half way upstairs when the phone rang again. I reached it and snatched it up before the tape could kick in.

'Hello?' I sounded croaky.

'Is that Sal?' A man's voice.

'Yes.'

'It's Stuart Bowker. We met the other night.'

'Oh, yes.' A blush washed my face and neck. Thank God he couldn't see me.

'I … well, I hope you don't mind me ringing. I got your number from Diane. I thought perhaps you might like to go for a meal sometime or to see a film or something.'

'Oh.' There was a horrible pause then we both spoke at once and both stopped. I tried again. 'Well, I'm not really up to it at the moment.' It sounded like a brush off. Was it? I couldn't work out what I felt except horribly embarrassed.

'OK,' he said, 'maybe some other time. I'll give you my number.'

'Right.' I had lost the power of articulate speech. He reeled it off but my biro wasn't working. I pressed down hard on the paper instead.

We said goodbyes. I replaced the receiver and groaned to myself. Before I could move away it rang. Him again?

'Hello?'

It was the police. Arranging to take my statement? I didn't catch what she was saying and had to ask her to repeat it.

'Your car, we've found your car, you reported it missing. Well, it's turned up over in Sharston. I'm afraid it's a write off, it's completely burnt out. They must have doused it with petrol and set fire to it.' She gave me the address, I scratched that on the paper.

I didn't have any great bond with my car, I never relished it or cherished it like some people do. None of my cars had ever had a name or been invested with a personality. A car was a car. I used it to get me, the kids and the shopping from A to B, that's all. So I was surprised at my reaction. I think the news had just come at a bad time. I put down the phone and burst into tears. I found a box of tissues and curled myself into the armchair in the corner of the kitchen and bawled for England. Quarter of an hour later, with a nose like Rudolph's, and only able to breathe with my mouth open, I disposed of all the crumpled tissues and packed away the first aid kit.

I heard the commotion as Ray, Tom and Maddie arrived back and took myself off to wash my face and put a dressing gown on. Using my teeth as well as my hand I managed to fashion a sling from an old scarf to reduce movement of my arm. When I joined them in the lounge Ray did a double take at my new injuries.

'What did you do, Mummy?'

'I burnt my leg,' I explained, 'and then I fell off my bike.'

Ray looked askance. What the fuck had I been doing on my bike?

'How did you burn it? Were you playing with matches?'

'Was it a bonfire?' cried Tom.

'Sort of.'

'Why weren't we there?'

My heart chilled at the thought.

'Oh, it wasn't a proper bonfire, just burning some old paper.' I didn't want to burden Maddie with the ugliness of the world. She already absorbed more than enough violence and misery via the news. I didn't want to have to explain why people had persecuted the Ibrahims, why they had burnt their house and slaughtered their son and killed another young man into the bargain. Eventually she would ask those sort of questions and I would do my best to explain, but not yet.

At four o'clock the police showed up and I spent a grim hour giving them a statement and answering their questions. They wouldn't tell me much about the case, only that they were making good progress and they were confident of being able to mount a prosecution. There would be an inquest, opened and adjourned until the Coroner's Office had completed their enquiries.

I felt drained when they had gone and went up to sleep, telling Ray that I would eat later. I missed Diane who called and left me a bunch of freesia. The kids were in bed though still awake so I said goodnight to them.

I reheated spicy chick peas and toasted some pitta bread. Clumsily I filled the bread with the chick peas and added some creamy yoghurt. It was good to eat.

The evening paper had come. The fire was front page news. 'Two dead in horror inferno.' And beneath it, 'Boy 6, and brave PC in arson tragedy'. Pictures of Carl Benson in his police uniform, a school photograph of the little boy, Mohammed Ismail Waberi, and another of the burnt out house.

There were quotes from the fire service about their hostile reception, the brutality of the arson attack and the rescue by onlookers (they mentioned both Johnny and I by name) and crew of Mrs Ahmed and the two younger children. Carl Benson's girlfriend was expecting their first child. A police spokesman mentioned the harassment the family had suffered and a council spokesperson sent condolences to the families involved and re-affirmed the council's determination to stamp out racial harassment and repossess tenancies from abusive tenants. A leader on the inside took up the issue.

I folded the paper up.

I could hear Ray hammering in the cellar. Someone had put the freesias in an old wine carafe. They were dwarfed. I found a smaller vase and transferred them. I couldn't smell them, my sense of smell was less than perfect with all the weeping and wailing I'd done and the effects of the smoke. But maybe they had no fragrance, hot house flowers often don't.

What now? I asked myself. I took the flowers into the lounge. I felt displaced, what would I do with the evening? Television didn't appeal and I knew I'd never be able to concentrate on a book. Chores would be nearly impossible with my injuries.

What now? My cases were over to all intents and purposes though there would be the inquest as well as the trial to attend. It would be months before there was any sense of closure on that and for the Ibrahims their loss would never end. Mrs Benson would bury her son Carl, and her grandchild would never meet its father; he would be a story, a handful of photographs, newspaper clippings, a hero.

With luck, people like Mandy Bellows and the lawyers in her section would get greater powers to act quickly in cases of racial harassment. Lessons would be learnt. With enough will, policies and practises in the police and health and education would change too. And perhaps for Maddie's generation things would be better, moving closer to the equal rights that any democracy must pursue.

And I had yet to tell Roger Pickering about Jennifer. Finally tell him where she had gone. Take away his hopes for a reunion. Kill her for him. And string his parents up beside her, accidental murderers. Destroy all his memories of growing up, corrupt the house and garden. Crucify him.

Or did I? I tried to imagine lying, colluding, denying all I knew but if I did the secret would haunt me, Jennifer would haunt me.

I would have to tell the police. Ask them to dig up the garden, find the proof. I could imagine the headlines; the press would go wild, comparing it to Fred and Rosemary West with their victims' bodies in the cellar, or the soap-opera Brookside with the corpse under the patio. The ripple of shock would spread around Jennifer's friends, Mrs Clerkenwell, the street.

At long last Roger would lay her bones to rest with proper ceremony. Hers and her child's. Her grave would be marked and known, her fate identified. I did not know whether Roger would ever exorcise her ghost, whether the nightmares of his family would fade and if he would find peace.

When Jennifer had a resting place I would take the little mosaic vase and place it there.

I cleared my plate away. No two cases are ever the same. There would be more work coming in. Safer work, I hoped. With happier outcomes. Tomorrow I had to get my dressing changed on my leg. I'd ask them to look at my arm too, just to make sure there was no infection. I would ring Roger and see how Mrs Pickering was. I'd prepare invoices for Roger and for Mandy Bellows.

I shuddered at the thought of passing him my bill on Monday and then devastating him with the truth. No, I'd post the bill on to him later. I'd have to sort out someone I could refer him to, he'd need support, tons of it, to weather what was coming.

And now?

It was tricky dialling but I got through straight away, the number that the pencil rubbing revealed was legible.

'It's Sal, I've been thinking it over. I'd like to do that, have a meal sometime. Can I ring you next week to fix it up?' By then I may be able to hold cutlery like a grown-up.

'Great. Yes, do. I'd like that.' He sounded delighted.

'OK. I'll do that, then. Bye bye.'

'Bye.'

I grinned and felt a cloud of butterflies rise in my belly.

The future beckoned.

The publishers hope that this book has given you enjoyable reading. Large Print Books are especially designed to be as easy to see and hold as possible. If you wish a complete list of our books please ask at your local library or write directly to:

Magna Large Print Books
Magna House, Long Preston,
Skipton, North Yorkshire.
BD23 4ND

This Large Print Book, for people
who cannot read normal print,
is published under the auspices of

THE ULVERSCROFT FOUNDATION

... we hope you have enjoyed this book.
Please think for a moment about those
who have worse eyesight than you ...
and are unable to even read or enjoy
Large Print without great difficulty.

You can help them by sending a
donation, large or small, to:

**The Ulverscroft Foundation,
1, The Green, Bradgate Road,
Anstey, Leicestershire, LE7 7FU,
England.**
or request a copy of our brochure for
more details.

The Foundation will use all donations
to assist those people who are visually
impaired and need special attention
with medical research, diagnosis
and treatment.

Thank you very much for your help.

3 4114 00466 2358

BLACKPOOL LIBRARY SERVICE